Shyness and Dignity

Dag Solstad

Shyness and Dignity

TRANSLATED
FROM THE NORWEGIAN
BY

Sverre Lyngstad

Harvill *Secker*
LONDON

Published by Harvill Secker, 2006

15

First published with the title *Genanse og verdighet*
by Forlaget Oktober, Oslo, 1999

First published in Great Britain in 2006 by
Harvill Secker
Random House, 20 Vauxhall Bridge Road
London SW1V 2SA

Random House Australia (Pty) Limited
20 Alfred Street, Milsons Point, Sydney,
New South Wales 2061, Australia

Random House New Zealand Limited
18 Poland Road, Glenfield,
Auckland 10, New Zealand

Random House South Africa (Pty) Limited
Isle of Houghton, Corner Boundary Road & Carse O'Gowrie,
Houghton 2198, South Africa

The Random House Group Limited Reg. No. 954009
www.randomhouse.co.uk/harvillsecker

A CIP catalogue record for this book is available from the British Library

ISBN 9781843432104

This book is published with the financial assistance of NORLA

Papers used by Random House are natural, recyclable products made
from wood grown in sustainable forests; the manufacturing processes conform to the
environmental regulations of the country of origin

Typeset in Bembo by SX Composing DTP, Rayleigh, Essex

Printed in Great Britain by Clays Ltd, St Ives plc

SHYNESS AND DIGNITY

H E WAS A RATHER sottish senior master in his fifties, with a wife who had spread out a bit too much and with whom he had breakfast every morning. This autumn day, too, a Monday in October, not yet knowing as he sat at the breakfast table with a light headache that it would be the decisive day in his life. Like every day, he had been careful to put on a sparkling white shirt, which alleviated the distaste he could not help feeling at having to live in such a time and under such conditions. He finished his breakfast in silence and looked out of the window, on to Jacob Aalls gate, as he had done innumerable times throughout the years. A street in Oslo, Norway's capital, where he lived and worked. It was a grey, oppressive morning, the sky was leaden, with scattered clouds drifting across it like black veils. I wouldn't be surprised if it rained, he thought, picking up his collapsible umbrella. He stuck it in his briefcase, together with his headache pills and some books. He bid a markedly cordial goodbye to his wife, in a tone that seemed genuine and sharply contrasted with his irritable, and her rather drawn, expression. But this is how it was every morning when he composed himself, with great difficulty, for this cordial 'take care of yourself', a gesture to this wife he had for years been living so close to and with whom he consequently had to feel a deep solidarity, and although he could now, on the whole, feel only remnants of this solidarity, it was essential for him to let her know every morning, by means of this cheerful and simple 'take care of yourself', that in his innermost heart he thought that nothing had changed between them, and while they both knew that it did not reflect the actual situation, he felt obliged to force himself, for the sake of propriety, to rise to a level high enough to make this gesture possible, not least because he then received a goodbye in return in the same simple and genuine tone, which had a soothing effect on his uneasiness and was indispensable to him. He walked to school, Fagerborg Secondary School, situated only seven or eight minutes from his home. His head felt heavy and he was a bit on edge, after drinking beer and aquavit the evening before, a little too much aquavit, about the right amount of beer, he thought. A little too much aquavit, which was now pressing on his forehead, like a chain. When he reached the school he went straight to the staff room, put away his briefcase, took out his books, swallowed a headache pill, said a brief but unaffected good morning to his colleagues, who had already taught one period, and went to his class.

He entered the classroom, closed the door behind him, and sat down behind the teacher's desk on the podium by the blackboard, which covered most of one long wall. Blackboard and chalk. Sponge. Twenty-five years in the service of the school. As he stepped into the classroom, the pupils hastily sat down at their desks. In front of him, twenty-nine young men and women about the age of eighteen who looked at him and returned his greeting. They removed their earpieces and put them in their pockets. He asked them to take out their school edition of *The Wild Duck*. He was once more struck by their hostile attitude towards him. But it could not be helped, he had a task to perform and was going through with it. It was from them as a group that he sensed the massive dislike sent forth by their bodies. Individually they could be very pleasant, but en bloc, positioned like now, at their desks, they constituted a structural enmity, directed at him and all that he stood for. Although they did as he told them. They took out their school edition of *The Wild Duck* without grumbling and placed it on their desks before them. He himself sat with an equivalent copy in front of him. *The Wild Duck* by Henrik Ibsen. This remarkable drama that Henrik Ibsen wrote at the age of fifty-six, in 1884. The class had been taken up with it for more than a month, and even so they were only in the middle of Act IV – that was doing things in style, he thought. A sleepy Monday morning. Norwegian class, actually a double period with a group of seniors, at Fagerborg Secondary School. Directly outside the windows, that grey, oppressive day. He was sitting behind his lectern, as he called it. The pupils with their noses and eyes turned towards the book. Some were slumped over rather than seated at their desks, which annoyed him, but he did not bother to take notice of it. He was speaking, holding forth. In the middle of Act IV. Where Mrs Sørbye appears in Ekdal's home and announces that she is going to marry Werle, the merchant, and where Ekdal's lodger Dr Relling is present, and he read (himself, instead of asking one of his pupils to do it, which he did at times for the sake of appearances, but he preferred to do it himself): 'Relling (with a slight tremor in his voice): This can't possibly be true? Mrs Sørbye: Yes, my dear Relling, indeed it is.' As he was reading he felt an unendurable excitement, because all at once he thought he was on the track of something to which he had not previously paid any attention when trying to understand *The Wild Duck.*

For twenty-five years he had gone through this drama by Henrik Ibsen with eighteen-year-olds in their last year of *gymnasium* (or secondary school), and he had always had problems with Dr Relling. He had not fully grasped what he was doing in the play. He had seen that his function was to proclaim elementary, unvarnished truths about the other characters in the play, well, actually about the entire play. He had seen him as a kind of mouthpiece for Ibsen and had been unable to grasp why that was necessary. Indeed, he had been of the opinion that the figure of Dr Relling weakened the play. What did Henrik Ibsen need a 'mouthpiece' for? Did not the play speak for itself? he had thought. But here, here there was something. Henrik Ibsen lays his hand on his minor character Dr Relling and, within parentheses, makes him speak with a slight tremor in his voice as he asks Mrs Sørbye if it is really true that she will marry Werle, the powerful merchant. For a moment, Henrik Ibsen pushes Relling into the drama he otherwise exclusively comments upon with his sarcasms. There he is, caught in his own bitter fate as a perpetual, unsuccessful admirer of Mrs Sørbye, throughout her two marriages, first to Dr Sørbye, now to Werle, and for a brief moment it is his fate, and nothing else, that is frozen into immobility on the stage. The moment of the minor figure. Both before and after this he remains the same, the man who reels off those smart lines, one of which has acquired an immortal status in Norwegian literature: 'If you take the life-lie away from an average person, you take away his happiness as well.'

It was this he now began to expatiate on to his pupils, who were partly sitting at, partly slumped over their desks. He asked them to flip their pages to Act III, where Dr Relling enters the stage for the first time, to read what he says there, and then move ahead to the end of Act IV (he assumed that the pupils were familiar with the whole play, although they had only reached the middle of Act IV in their examination of it, for their first assignment had been to read the play in its entirety, which he presumed they had done, regardless of what the pupils themselves, individually or as a whole, had accomplished in that respect, thinking, with the hint of an inward smile flickering through his rather – after yesterday's meditative little drinking bout – shivery body, that there was no reason why he should act as a policeman in class), the very place where Dr Relling, among other things, utters his subsequently immortalised statement about the life-lie, and he said: There you can see, Dr Relling is just chattering, all the time, except for one place, and that is where we are right now. Now we've got him, you see, he is in the drama for the first and last time. The pupils did as they were told, leafed back, leafed forward, leafed back to where they were, namely, where they had Dr Relling in the drama for the first and last time. Did they yawn? No, they did not yawn; why should they yawn, this was not something that called for a demonstration so violent as to necessitate a yawn, this was a perfectly ordinary Norwegian class for a group of seniors one Monday morning at Fagerborg Secondary School. There they sat, listening to the teacher's interpretation of a play that was a prescribed text for their final examination in Norwegian, *The Wild Duck*, named after a wild duck that lived in an attic, a dark attic as it happened, some looking at the page, some at him, some out of the window. The minutes were slowly ticking away. The teacher continued to talk about the made-up character Dr Relling, who seems to have spoken an immortal line in a play by Ibsen. Here he is, he said, frozen firmly to his own bitter fate. Bitter for him, on the verge of the ridiculous for the rest of us, not least if we were to have him presented to us by way of Dr Relling's own sarcasms.

But, he added, and now he pointed his finger straight at the class, which startled a few of them, because they did not like to be pointed at in that way, what would have happened if this scene had not been included? Nothing. The play would have been exactly the same, apart from the fact that Dr Relling would not have had his quivering moment. Because it is completely superfluous. It does not affect the development of the plot in the least, nor does it change, as we have seen, Dr Relling, the minor figure. He is exactly the same character, with exactly the same function, both before and after his quivering moment. And when we know that this play is written by the masterful Henrik Ibsen, who carefully lays out his characters and scenes and leaves nothing to chance, we have to ask: Why does Ibsen include this superfluous scene, where Dr Relling, a minor character, speaks a line 'with a slight tremor in his voice' and is suddenly pulled into the play as someone with a destiny? There has to be a reason, and since the scene is superfluous, well, in reality, wasted, there can be no other reason than that Ibsen wants to show this made-up minor character of his, Dr Relling, a handsome gesture. But then the question arises: Why . . .? In that moment, however, the bell rang and the pupils instantly straightened up, closed their school editions of *The Wild Duck*, got up and walked quietly and confidently out of the classroom, past the teacher, whom they did not take notice of for a moment, not a single one of them, and who was now sitting on his chair, all by himself, annoyed at having been interrupted in the middle of a question.

Ten years ago, he thought, as he too got up, they would at least have let him get to the end of his sentence. But now, as soon as the school bell rang, they closed their books and left the classroom, confidently and blame-lessly, because it was beyond doubt that the ringing of the bell signalled the end of the period. The decision was made by the bell, such were the rules whereby the instruction was organised, and one had to follow the rules, they would have said, calmly and convincingly, if he had said it was he who decided when the period was over. They would have looked at him and asked, Why, then, do we have a bell that rings when, after all, it is you and not the bell that decides? he thought they would have said. Then it would have been useless for him to mention that the bell was simply a means of reminding a teacher that it was time to stop, in case he became so fervently elated by his teaching that he forgot both time and place. He went towards the staff room. He was a bit irritated. Not least because he had looked forward to the break even more than they, and he certainly needed it more, tired as he was, both beforehand and after talking for three quarters of an hour almost without a stop. He needed a glass of water and he needed a headache pill. And as he stood there in front of the drinking fountain and poured cold water into a glass, sneaked out a pill and swallowed it, he thought that, by Jove, just the way I feel right now, Dr Relling must have felt throughout the play, with a pressure on his forehead, all shivery, slightly weary of body and soul, yes, it was precisely in this condition he found himself as he went about uttering his semi-elegant (yes, he had to admit that was the way he viewed them) lines, of which at least one had been made immortal, and he had to smile to himself. He sat down in his usual place at the large table in the staff room and talked a little with his colleagues about the football results over the weekend etc. Since the teachers were originally from widely different parts of Norway, every team in our two upper divisions was represented by at least one fervent fan, and those who had won over the weekend never failed to make everyone aware of it. He himself was in Division III, at the top of the division, to be sure, with an annual hope of moving up to Division II, but when they asked him questions it was still mostly out of politeness and sympathy, which he could not find any fault with. (His female colleagues did not take part in these discussions, though they sat at the same table, beside the men, but they were knitting, as he used to tell his wife with a sly little laugh.)

Then back to the classroom. But why should Ibsen offer this gesture to his mouthpiece? he asked, even before the last pupils had come in, found their seats and closed the door. That I cannot understand, it seems so unnecessary, even self-contradictory, well, almost like poor dramatic thinking, and therefore we have to call into question whether Dr Relling is Ibsen's mouthpiece at all in this play. One reason for Dr Relling to serve as Ibsen's mouthpiece must, after all, be to prevent Gregers Werle from getting off too easily. But does Gregers Werle get off so easily? It is he, we know, who asks Hedvig to sacrifice herself, shoot and kill the wild duck, and who thus triggers the tragedy. He triggers the tragedy, and is at the same time preoccupied with the idea that Hjalmar Ekdal grows in moral stature as a result. Grows owing to the tragedy that he, Gregers Werle, is responsible for having triggered. Is that not sufficient? One would certainly think so. No, Dr Relling is needed for Gregers Werle to get his comeuppance. But what, then, is Dr Relling's function in the play, as a minor figure to whom Ibsen even offers the unnecessary gesture that turns him, in a quivering moment, into a frozen destiny, supposed to be? Well, if one reads the play with one's eyes open, without thinking of anything but just this, and then asks the question, When is Dr Relling necessary? the answer is obvious. Dr Relling is necessary in one place, and that is near the end of the last act. He asked the pupils to leaf forward, and they did, some quickly, others slowly, all sitting in that same dim light which is characteristic of classrooms in a Norwegian school. He also leafed forward and read the scene, in which a shot is heard from inside the attic. A little later it becomes clear that Hedvig has fired the pistol and that the shot has hit herself. What has happened? Has she, at Gregers Werle's request, gone there to shoot the winged wild duck, fumbled around with the pistol and shot herself? A terrible accident, but profound tragedy? No, this is no accidental shot, the twelve-year-old child has aimed the pistol at herself and pulled the trigger. To show this, to elevate the play from a banal accident to a shocking tragedy, that is, Ibsen needs a character with the authority to confirm that this is the case. In other words, Ibsen needs a physician. Dr Relling, he exclaimed, pounding the table in a flurry of elation. The pupils gave a start, some looking at him in puzzlement, a couple even knitting their brows, as he thought he noticed. Ibsen needs Dr Relling as a natural authority, a witness to the truth, so that he can write this: 'Dr Relling (goes over to Gregers and says): No-one shall ever fool me into thinking that this was an accident. Gregers (who has stood horror-stricken, twitching convulsively): Nobody can know for certain how this terrible thing happened. Relling: The wadding has burned her bodice. She must have pressed the pistol straight at her breast and fired. Gregers: Hedvig has not died in vain. Didn't you see how grief released the greatness in him?'

Here, and only here, is Dr Relling necessary. It is on account of this scene that he is in the play. But when Ibsen needs a physician, a doctor, at the end of his drama, he cannot simply have him pop up from nowhere, he must have been introduced to us before. And so we have been thinking that he walks in and out of Ibsen's play as 'Ibsen's mouthpiece'. But what does he do, in reality? Well, he offers a continuous commentary on the play. He comes out with characterisations of the dramatis personae, and he also comments on the action. As a commentator, Ibsen has worked him into his drama. And what kind of comments does Dr Relling bring to bear? They all point unequivocally in one and the same direction. That so and so is a fool, that so and so has been a dunce all his life, that so and so is a naive nitwit, that so and so is a pompous and unbearable rich man's son who suffers from a morbid sense of justice. All of them simple, cynical, even banal truths. And these banal truths are showered upon the characters in Ibsen's drama, mind you, as this drama is being performed. Dr Relling drags the whole play into the mud. Far from being Ibsen's mouthpiece, Dr Relling is the play's enemy, since all he says has only one purpose: to destroy it, to destroy this drama which Henrik Ibsen is writing. Hjalmar Ekdal is a deceived fool, leave him and his family alone. Gregers Werle, however, does not leave him alone, and Dr Relling says that Gregers Werle is a fool as well, morbidly egocentric on other people's behalf – that is what I think anyway, the person sitting on the podium added with a little embarrassed smile, and all that he, Gregers Werle, can manage to create is a dismal misery we should all have been spared. The daughter in the family, a twelve-year-old girl, takes her own life, Hjalmar Ekdal is still a big puffed-up fool, and Gregers Werle is exposed, not unexpectedly, as a cold fish who keeps drooling about 'the depths of the sea', he added, almost astounded at himself and his words, so that, when Hedvig is dead, he can only think about whether Hjalmar Ekdal bears his grief with real dignity. Honestly, can this be anything to write a drama about! he cried out, again evoking disapproving glances from some of his pupils, while others were half slumped over, half sitting at their desks in transparent composure and drowsiness. Not if Dr Relling is right, he said, lowering his voice, and Dr Relling is perfectly right, after all, as everybody can see, even Ibsen himself, who can by no means be ignorant of the fact that Dr Relling expresses his own 'opinions' of the characters he is writing about. All the same, Ibsen goes on writing, because there is something that Dr Relling *cannot* have seen, and that is what makes the famous fifty-six-year-old dramatist go on writing. Dr Relling is Henrik Ibsen's antagonist. It is Dr Relling versus Dr Ibsen. Henrik Ibsen writes doggedly on, and he gives Dr Relling everything, he even lets him have the last word, he explained, gesticulating wildly. And why? he quickly added, as he collected himself. Yes, why? We have to remember that it is Dr Relling versus Dr Ibsen, to be sure, but it is Dr Ibsen who invents or creates Dr

Relling. He exists nowhere else than in the moment Dr Ibsen writes 'Dr Relling' on a piece of paper and lets him utter some of those semi-elegant home truths which threaten to tear this whole drama to pieces. Why does Ibsen do this? he asked. Why, why? he asked, looking out at the class, which offered no traceable response; on the contrary, it formed, in a faceted way, by dint of an array of different body languages and facial expressions, a compact and impenetrable hostile entity that once more made him realise that to sit here and let himself be carried away by his interpretation of *The Wild Duck* and of Dr Relling, a minor character, was a torture.

It was not that they were bored, it was rather that look of injury through which their boredom became manifest. There was nothing strange about being bored in a Norwegian class where a drama by Henrik Ibsen was being studied. They were, after all, eighteen-year-olds who were supposed to acquire a liberal education. They were youths who could not be viewed as fully developed individuals. To characterise them as immature, therefore, would not offend anyone, neither themselves nor those with authority over them, at any rate when considered from a sober and objective viewpoint. These immature individuals were placed in school in order to obtain knowledge about classical Norwegian literature, which it was his job to offer them. He was, in fact, officially appointed to do just that. The main problem with such a job was that they were incapable of receiving what he was supposed to give them. Immature individuals, at that in and of itself exciting stage between child and adult, are not in a position to understand *The Wild Duck* by Henrik Ibsen; to maintain anything else would be an insult to the old master, and for that matter to every grown-up person who has managed to obtain some knowledge of the shared cultural heritage of humanity. That was why, at this educational level, one spoke of pupils, not students. They were not students who were supposed to study, they were pupils who were there to learn. He was the teacher, they were pupils. However, since this was the highest level of general education in Norway, certain demands were made on the quality of what was to be taught there. This meant that what was to be conveyed was not always immediately adapted to the pupils' uncultivated intellectual and emotional life, but was often of a kind that went over their heads, so that they actually had to stretch, and vigorously too, simply in order to see what was being communicated to them. There was general agreement that pupils who had completed the highest level of general education offered in Norway ought to have a certain knowledge of the Norwegian cultural heritage, not least as it has been preserved in literature, and so, here he was this rainy Monday morning at the Fagerborg school, dutifully going through a drama by Henrik Ibsen. They were to become familiar with it, but since this work obviously went over their heads at the immature stage of their lives where they found themselves, it was unavoidable that tedium settled on the classroom. That was how it had always been, it was built into the instruction, its method and goal – indeed, he had himself been bored in his *gymnasium* Norwegian classes, and as soon as he had stepped into the classroom as a fledgling teacher, seven years later, he had immediately recognised the same boredom among the pupils, whom he now was to teach a subject which he himself had considered boring when he was in school, a situation that, accordingly, is part and parcel of the conditions which govern the acquisition of general knowledge in youth, and which the one who is to communicate this knowledge must relate to with, as it were, a cheerful heart, just as he had done for at least the first fifteen or twenty years of his tenure in secondary school. He had even been amused at the thought that his teaching bored the pupils, thinking, Well, such is life, that's the way it is, and must be, to teach in secondary school in a civilised country. The very thought of the contrary situation sufficed to make one quickly understand how impossible it would have been if it had not been the way it, as a matter of fact, was. Just try to imagine what things would be like if the cultural heritage awakened an enormous enthusiasm among the coming generation, so that they devoured it greedily, because it had both the questions and the answers to what they had secretly been preoccupied with – a sweet thought in a way, but not if one considers the reality of the situation, namely, that it is a question of immature people with a rather confused, incomplete, even at times directly commonplace emotional and intellectual life. If the literature handed down to us through our cultural heritage really took hold of our youth, at the mental and psychological level where it finds itself, that would, if true, throw a painful light on the very culture which called this literature 'our cultural heritage'.

Further, it would have to mean that the essays the pupils presented to their teacher, in this instance the one sitting at his desk in a classroom at Fagerborg Secondary School in Oslo this rainy, leaden Monday morning, were veritable literary dissertations, which he could barely refrain from pouncing on until he had got home, not to correct but to *read*, which was so far from the actual state of affairs as anything could be, indeed it was a phantom, a figment of the imagination, to put it mildly, something he knew very well after dutifully struggling through his pupils' unfinished intellectual creations for all of twenty-five years, with at least three piles of essays every single month. No, the literature of the cultural heritage did not succeed in awakening the enthusiasm of the young, and their essays were not dissertations on a level with the outstanding achievements of the cultural heritage. And so we were left with the actual situation: the tedium that envelops Norwegian classrooms when the teacher goes through a dramatic work by Henrik Ibsen with his pupils. A tedium which does not even spare the teacher. For twenty-five years he had taught the same works by Ibsen, by and large, and it cannot be denied that he often felt as though he were regurgitating the same stuff, over and over again. He abhorred the first words in *Peer Gynt*, with the lines, 'Peer, you're lying', 'No, I'm not', similarly 'The Buckride', something he was careful not to let his pupils in on. Only rarely did he derive as much personal pleasure from teaching as he did today. On the whole, what he presented to his pupils were quite well-known and, to him, elementary exegeses which were not capable of arousing his interest. True, it would happen that he began with a rather well-known thesis, for example, the similarity between Hjalmar Ekdal and Peer Gynt, and between Brand and Gregers Werle, and that he managed to express himself in a way that once more made him take an interest in this double comparison, felt inspired and had a sense that he glimpsed something, said something he had never thought before, but it was very seldom. But today he had. Quite unexpectedly. Oh, this Dr Relling, he had thought, with a deep mental sigh, when he asked his pupils to open their school editions of *The Wild Duck* to page forty-three and did the same himself. That perpetual mouthpiece. But then, just because Dr Relling in this scene on page forty-three, through the parenthetical 'with a slight tremor in his voice', had become part of Ibsen's drama, it had suddenly dawned on him that Dr Relling was not the play's rather uninteresting mouthpiece, because then, then Ibsen, the old master, would not have stooped so low as to give his voice a slight tremor and thus worked him into this little scene with Mrs Sørbye, where he appears as a dramatic character, with his bitter fate as a perpetual admirer of this, for the reader's part, not all-too-attractive widow Mrs Sørbye, and he had again felt inspired. But naturally his eloquence and inspiration had no chance of awakening his pupils, who were, after all in no position to understand him. His eloquence could only inspire himself, while his pupils were bound, by their very nature, to continue partly to slump over, partly to sit at their desks, enduring the usual tedium of their instruction in the literature of their mother tongue. It was he alone, the teacher, who for once escaped the suffocating tedium of Norwegian class, making him feel very satisfied with himself at the end of the period. But it was an entirely trifling feeling which applied only to himself and not them, who were, after all, in no position to be happy about it, although he might hope that some were at least surprised to hear him so elated in the midst of this tedious grind of going through a work by Ibsen. But even if a few individuals among the immature group really were thus surprised, that too was, in the big scheme of things, a trifling (though happy) event. His task was plainly not that of producing inspiring exegeses of the great works of the national literature, his task was quite simply, within the framework of this classroom and through a certain number of repeated periods a week over three years, to form these immature pupils of his and enable them to understand certain requirements which this nation, and this civilisation, was based on, and which both he, the adult teacher, and they, his young and rather confused and unfinished pupils, were part of. It was the fact that he, a grown, very well-educated man, had been placed in this classroom, at public expense, in order to go through, for the twenty-fifth year, a certain number of literary works from our common cultural heritage, whether the pupils were bored or not: it was this that directed his efforts. It was this that made him, the occasional radiance or lack of radiance of his humble person, his ability to inspire or his deficient ability to inspire notwithstanding, into a commanding presence who, in the short or long run, effected that formation of them which society had placed him there to accomplish. For that reason the pupils' boredom had not touched him, not until now, lately, because it was caused merely by the fact that they were immature and inadequate, and this boredom was experienced both by him and the pupils (until *now*) as a lack. And this lack would mark them later in life. Either because they eliminated it or, and this applied to the majority, because unconsciously it marked their educated speech, which showed a socially determined lack in their full-grown personality. He had often experienced this when, for example, he met old friends from the *gymnasium* and told them in the course of conversation that he was studying Norwegian literature at the university – this was when they were in their twenties, the period in which he had most often come across old friends from high school – or he told them that he was a senior master at Fagerborg and made a point of studying Ibsen's plays with his pupils; it was then that the other would say, Oh, Ibsen, well, I'm afraid he's over my head, or, Hm, you know, I never became interested in literature, and in this there was a regret, and it was not their own, for they, after all, were so little interested in literature and in Ibsen's plays that they saw no reason to regret anything; what in heaven's name was there to regret, as far as they were concerned? No, it was as social beings that they found it necessary to express this regret, namely, a regret that was a necessary expression of the cultural background which every civilised society seeks to impart to its citizens and which, as one can see, it had in this instance succeeded in doing. That simple conversations between old acquaintances who meet by chance after some years turn out like that and not in the exactly opposite way, on this every civilised society builds its foundations, he had often thought, not least in the last few years.

But the young people who were now, on this particular day, a rainy Monday in early October, sitting opposite him, in this damp classroom in Norway's capital city, and were bored by his exegesis of Henrik Ibsen's drama *The Wild Duck*, were bored in an entirely different way than previously. He could not recognise his own boredom from secondary school in them, not at all, and he could not recognise the boredom of drowsy class hours on Henrik Ibsen that had marked previous sets of pupils, down to just a few years ago. The young people who now sat here in all their immaturity, being bored by his elated interest in Dr Relling's function in *The Wild Duck*, did not look at their boredom as a natural consequence of being a pupil; on the contrary, they were indignant at actually having to spend this Monday morning being bored in Norwegian class at Fagerborg Secondary School, despite the fact, which they could not disregard, that they were, after all, pupils in this school and accordingly had to turn up. There they sat with their soft, puppyish, youthful faces, their – as they thought – horrible pimples, and with a confused and inadequate inner life filled as likely as not with the most soapy daydreams, actually feeling offended because they were bored, and he was the one they were offended by, because it was he, the teacher, who was boring them. And that was an affront that could not be blown away by a friendly remark like, Oh, don't act so offended, Cathrine, or, Try to pretend you're interested anyway, Anders Christian. For they were deeply offended. It was not just skin-deep but had completely saturated them, having become their dominant and fundamental attitude towards him, and thus their funda- mental attitude as pupils in a classroom in which one of the foremost dramatic works of our literature was being studied. They quite simply felt victimised, and that was not to be disposed of lightly. Being bored was such an unendurable experience to them that their bodies, the bodies of absolutely everyone, and their faces, those of boys and girls alike, whether bright or less so, those good in school as well as those who just sat (or lay) there to pass the time, expressed a pent-up indignation. Why should they put up with this? How long should they put up with it? Does he have the right to do this to us? That, he could see, was what they were thinking.

There were, no doubt, some among them who were more tolerant than others and who, while sharing their fellow pupils' sense of being treated unfairly, never- theless tried to take a broad view and thus had a moderating effect on the others. They expressed the view that it was only a matter of time before such a method of teaching Ibsen would be a thing of the past, that in other words he was hopelessly old-fashioned and that, consequently, they ought to stretch a point and wink at him, and thanks to these pupils the pent-up indignation was mitigated in favour of a more traditional expression of general tedium, in any case seemingly. But although the classroom situation could in this way appear ever so jovial in all its drowsiness, he knew he was in reality unwanted as a teacher among his pupils, which in itself caused him no more pain than an average emotional hurt experienced by anyone not feeling expressly welcome somewhere; but since, in addition, those who did not welcome him as a teacher considered themselves perfectly justified, he felt deeply depressed now and then, because it made him look like someone who just stuck around, though his time was up, a hopeless, old-fashioned teacher, obsolete and spent, whereas at other times this irritation made him feel a certain ardour stir inside him that positively gave him courage. He would stand the way he stood, erect, and let his pupils have a chance to stretch towards Ibsen and the rest of their cultural heritage; while falling short at present, they would do better later in life.

His pupils behaved the way they did as a matter of course. They were not for a moment in doubt that when they did not rise to protest against his instruction, it was due exclusively to their own kind-heartedness and magnanimity. They were convinced without question that he could continue on his course solely at their pleasure. He sat there at their pleasure. Of this, his young, immature pupils were convinced, and if they were capable of such a conviction, it could not possibly be due to their own incomplete life and inadequate level of development, but to something wholly outside themselves. And so they were not themselves to blame, but in any case it was a quite detestable situation to be in for a well-educated grown man, with twenty-five years of experience in teaching his country's mother tongue. Dr Relling. Dr Relling, the minor figure. Naturally, there were among the best pupils some who not only reacted to the fact that his teaching did not concern them, but also to his permitting himself to waste their precious time, as pupils with an eye on their final examination, by forcing them to occupy themselves with a minor figure in a play by Henrik Ibsen, though as required reading the play was otherwise relevant enough. Just as, among the brightest of them, there were some who felt that the teacher *could* have made it more interesting by paying attention to the literary history they were also reading. There it said that Henrik Ibsen anticipated the detective novel by his retrospective technique in shaping the dramatic action. Anticipating the detective story, could not that have been something? In any case, it would have been something for them. Others felt it was odd that he did not seize his chance to make Ibsen a little more relevant to the topics of the day, such as suicide, since, after all, Hedvig did commit suicide, as far as they understood. Why could he not have taken that as his starting point, since today it is a real problem that so many young people commit suicide? But not even that. Dr Relling. Dr Relling, the minor figure. Oh, if only the teacher could have said, It's not true that Ibsen is a dusty old classic. The truth is that he is almost as suspenseful as a detective story. And then he could have explained in what way Ibsen was almost as suspenseful as a detective novel. Then he would have given them something of potential concern to them.

But no. The teacher dealt with classical Norwegian

literature on the express premise that it was classical Norwegian literature they were now being given, within the framework of a Norwegian public school, which was to lead them, eighteen-year-olds with round cheeks, to the highest level of general education the country was able to give its youth. He talked. About Dr Relling, a minor figure in the play *The Wild Duck* he was now absorbed by, as – if he might say so – he had a right to be as a senior master in Norwegian to a graduating class at Fagerborg Secondary School. This was the third of four plays by Ibsen they had to study. They had read *Peer Gynt* and *Brand* already, and after *The Wild Duck* they would read either *Ghosts* or *Hedda Gabler* (he had not yet decided which, taking great pleasure every year in weighing pros and cons of any fourth play of Ibsen's to be included in the syllabus, *Hedda Gabler*, *Ghosts*, *Rosmersholm*, or *When We Dead Awaken*). As a result his pupils got a lot of Ibsen, more than those who had other teachers, who as a rule stopped at one play (*Peer Gynt*), or at most two. That did not mean that he passed over Bjørnstjerne Bjørnson, Kielland, Jonas Lie. Well, he did pass over Lie a bit, being of the opinion that the ravages of time had so severely eroded Jonas Lie that he could no longer defend his place among the Four Greats, and so he would rather not let his pupils read him but gave Lie's place to Garborg, so that one (i.e., he) could still talk about the Four Greats, who now, accordingly, were Bjørnson, Ibsen, Kielland, Garborg (though when all was said and done he considered neither Bjørnson, Kielland or Garborg really to be among the Four Greats, the four really great being Ibsen, Hamsun,

Vesaas, Mykle, but these were thoughts and ideas which carried him far away from the classroom where he had his day's work and did his duty, although he had actually wished all along that one of his pupils would pose precisely this question. That, after he had mentioned that the Four Greats in Norwegian literature must now probably be said to be Ibsen, Bjørnson, Kielland, Garborg, when for almost one hundred years one had considered it to be Ibsen, Bjørnson, Kielland, Lie, the time having come for letting Garborg occupy Lie's place in order to prevent the breakdown of the very concept of the Four Greats, some bright eighteen-year-old would hold up his hand and ask, But master, master, does that mean that the Four Greats are your favourites? which he then would have had the opportunity to deny: No, no, my favourites are Ibsen, Hamsun, Vesaas, Mykle. But as [in his daydreams] he would have a chance to say exactly this, he would have hastened to add, But you must not attach great importance to that, because when I express myself that way I speak like a limited person, like a captive of my own time; my statement betrays how easily my heart is moved by literature from my own century rather than how good my judgment is at rendering valid appraisals of our national literature in general, he would say if he had been posed this question by a bright, extremely eager eighteen-year-old, and by this reply he hoped he would have been able to convey an aspect of himself that the pupils might be surprised he had, for he could vividly imagine [he dreamed] that it would astonish his pupils that he too, after all, let himself be moved more easily by contemporary literature than by the literature of earlier periods – that was what he imagined they thought when he was giving a sincere answer to a question asked by a bright and interested hypothetical eighteen-year-old pupil, and then they would perhaps understand that when there was such a dearth of contemporary literature in his classes, it was not due to his personal taste, but to an overarching plan, the nature of which would now, right now, he thought as he was thinking about this hypothetical situation, dawn on them, like a sudden glimpse of something that was of greater importance than both they themselves, the pupils, and the one who was teaching them, the master). So, Bjørnson, Kielland, Garborg, beside Ibsen. One work by each, every year. These were the Four Greats. Next, the great writers before them. Norse literature. Folk ballads. Petter Dass. Holberg. Wessel. Wergeland and Welhaven (and not the way it has usually been: Wergeland [and Welhaven]). Ivar Aasen. Vinje. Amalie Skram. From the twentieth century: Olaf Bull. Kinck. Hamsun. Vesaas. Not Mykle; one must at least die before making one's entry into the schools. That was all. Nobody forgotten? Yes, Obstfelder. No-one else? He could not entirely bypass Sigrid Undset, but his appetite for going through *Kristin Lavransdatter* was rather limited; he preferred Cora Sandel. But then full stop. No contemporary literature, except to exemplify classical literature, language development, thematic changes, etc., throughout the ages.

This was how he taught the literature of his mother tongue. This was how it went from year to year. For the pupils a steady grind, which in some might arouse a bit of curiosity, if only to understand why a grown-up, well-educated man could have, as his official occupation, the job of sitting behind a desk in a classroom bidding young people to read all these books they were neither particularly interested in nor understood to any great extent, not the way this officially appointed educator tried to make them read them anyway, books that were intended for everybody regardless of whether they were grazed by such a curiosity, which could of course be the first condition for *making an effort*, so that those who, despite everything, had received their society's highest general education as nineteen-year-olds would not later in life in their everyday conversation – the sum of which, with its different nuances and under- and overtones, forms society's own self-understanding – serve up private gush and loose talk about topics worthy of a more seemly demeanour, thereby demonstrating that even among those who had received society's highest education there were downright uncivilised individuals who did not even have sufficient breeding to hide it, let alone be ashamed of it, he had thought; but this was before the present situation had dawned on him. He had taken his teaching seriously, and often the routine aspect of it had been trying for him, but short of making him feel it was no longer meaningful to teach your mother tongue, and especially its belles-lettres, its beautiful literature, as he jokingly called it at times to his colleagues, and not on account of the few classes in which he seemed to succeed in getting on to something new in the work he was presenting to his pupils, for they were the exceptions, no matter how stimulating, joyful, even brilliant, if he might say so, and they were not a condition for finding his existence to be meaningful. All the more enjoyable it was when such classes occurred. Like now. In this double period on a rainy day in early October, for the graduating seniors. He was on the track of something now. Something having to do with what Ibsen was really struggling with when he wrote *The Wild Duck*, well, what he was actually looking for. Based on the assumption that Dr Relling is Ibsen's antagonist and that Dr Relling is right, or 'right'. No, right. He once more asked the pupils to turn their pages to the end of the play. They did, automatically, grudgingly, without a murmur. He asked one of the pupils to read from where it says, 'Relling (goes up to Gregers and says): 'No-one shall ever fool me into thinking . . .' The pupil, an overgrown boy dressed in the latest fashion and enveloped in the most profound boredom, read tonelessly and so carelessly that he did not even bother to caricature his own voice to create a bit of 'life' or 'mood', a little 'fun and laughter' in the classroom – not for a moment did he succumb to the temptation to respond to the boredom with a touch of tomfoolery, which would have been natural and often happened in earlier days, he recalled; no, he preferred, as a striking expression of the attitude of his class, to suffer in silence, secure in his conviction, his faith in the future, that it was only a question of time when exhausted and extinct phenomena would no longer form part of the required curriculum for a liberal education, not on this side of the globe at any rate. 'Relling (goes up to Gregers and says): No-one shall ever fool me into thinking that this was an accident. Gregers (who has stood horror-stricken, twitching convulsively): Nobody can say for certain how this terrible thing happened. Relling: The wadding has burned her bodice. She must have pressed the pistol straight at her breast and fired. Gregers: Hedvig has not died in vain. Didn't you see how grief released the greatness in him? Relling: Most people show a certain greatness when they stand grieving over a dead body. But how long, do you think, this nobility of his will last? Gregers: Why shouldn't it last and grow all his life! Relling: Within nine months little Hedvig will be nothing more to him than a fine pretext for speechifying. Gregers: You dare say that about Hjalmar Ekdal! Relling: We'll talk again when the first grass has withered on her grave. Then you will hear him spouting phrases like 'the child prematurely torn from the paternal bosom', then you can watch him wallowing in sentiment, self-admiration and self-pity. Wait and see! Gregers: If *you* are right and *I* am wrong, life is not worth living.' Thanks, he said, and the pupil instantly stopped his toneless reading. That's it, he burst out. What we've been looking for. Don't you see, Dr Relling is right, you can see that! Of course, Dr Relling is right, we could all of us have said the same thing, it's to the point. And yet, the drama is that of Gregers Werle. It's what *he* says that makes the play tick, he said, for some reason or other, he had perhaps meant to say kick or stick. He grew slightly embarrassed at this 'tick', which had fallen out of his mouth. Yes, 'tick,' he repeated, for what does Gregers

Werle say? Well, he says, If Dr Relling is right, what we are doing here is not worthwhile, and Dr Relling is right, after all, but so what? Well, what he says, damn it, he exclaimed. What Gregers Werle says is the drama, after all! What has Gregers Werle not done? He has killed Hedvig, lured her, seduced her with words, to carry out this sacrifice. Hedvig, this half-blind child, in puberty, with a pistol in her hand inside an absurd dark attic to make a sacrifice, suddenly understands that it is not the wild duck, but *herself* she must give to her father, about whom she too has her doubts, being uncertain whether he *is* her father or not, but she is his daughter unto death all the same, about that she has no doubts, so why the wild duck when she has herself, unto death herself, to give away? And then she does it! The shot is fired. Now he certainly must understand that he is her father and that she loves him. What cruelty is hidden in the depths of this play, he exclaimed. An elder brother driving his little sister to her death, and afterwards he needs to see the imagined father experience a *sincere* sorrow, for otherwise life is not worth living. Gregers Werle is shuddering, both at his own deed and at the possibility that Dr Relling is right. And Dr Relling is right, but it is Gregers Werle's shudders which are . . . which are . . . He searched desperately for words. He was on the track now, but he could not find the right word for it. He had it on the tip of his tongue, but did not find it. He was in despair, but not because, as a teacher, he was unable to give so brilliant an interpretation of *The Wild Duck* as he thought he could *see* in his mind's eye. That, he felt, was fully compensated for by the fact that the pupils had now had the rare opportunity, he would not hesitate to say good fortune, of observing, in close-up, a grown man struggle with the absolutely essential questions of our cultural legacy in an acceptable, though imperfect, way, making him stammer, perspire, follow certain trains of thought as far as he, in his incomplete manner, was capable of doing, and if that was not sufficient to cause the nostrils of at least some of his pupils to start *sensing* some of the conditions which their lives, too, would build on, as a foundation, and even if they might never read this play by Henrik Ibsen again, they would still understand the reasons why this play was present here, now. No, his despair was due solely to his not finding the words he was searching for, which he thought were so near, but when he wanted to get at them, and pronounce them, they were not there, except for a rather useless, miserable surrogate, which might be somewhat similar, as far as it went, but not at all what he had been looking for and even thought he had found. Terrible, he burst out, we will have to do it once more.

He asked one of the pupils, an eighteen-year-old girl, to read it again. She bends over the book and begins to read. But at that very moment a resigned sigh is heard from one of the other pupils, who is no longer capable of sup-pressing it. Loud and clear, on the verge of a savage roar, so insolent that it made him give an inward start, but despite the fact that the class peeked cautiously up at him, on the sly, he chose to ignore it and waved the eighteen-year-old girl on. She read. A teenager with a dreary, rather bashful face and sweet, calf-like voice that seemed to search for the words, which she recited somewhat unsteadily and fumblingly, either because she did not understand what she was reading, or because a layer of dew had coated her eyelashes, brought about by an unendurable and glaringly unjust drowsiness that was blinding her like tears, so that she could not see clearly but had to look for the words, one by one. 'Relling (goes up to Gregers and says): No-one shall ever fool me into thinking that this was an accident. Gregers (who has stood horror-stricken, twitching convulsively): Nobody can say for certain how this terrible thing happened. Relling: The wadding has burned her bodice. She must have pressed the pistol straight at her breast and fired. Gregers: Hedvig has not died in vain. Did you not see how grief released the greatness in him? Relling: Most people show a certain greatness when they stand grieving over a dead body. But how long, do you think, this nobility of his will last? Gregers: Why shouldn't it last and grow all his life! Relling: Within nine months little Hedvig will be nothing more to him than a fine pretext for speechifying. Gregers: You dare say that about Hjalmar Ekdal! Relling: We'll talk again when the first grass has withered on her grave. Then you will hear him spouting phrases like "the child prematurely torn from the paternal bosom", then you can watch him wallowing in sentiment, self-admiration and self-pity. Wait and see! Gregers: If *you* are right and *I* am wrong, life is not worth living. Relling: Oh, life can still be quite alright, if only we could be left alone by these damn bill collectors who force themselves on poor people with this so-called claim of the ideal. Gregers (with a vacant look in his eyes): In that case I'm glad my destiny is what it is. Relling: What, then, is your destiny, if I may ask? Gregers (about to leave): To be the thirteenth at table. Relling: The hell it is.'

He listened to this rather stammering reading with increasing irritation and became completely paralysed. Not because of the reading, but because of the aggressive, suppressed groan heard in the classroom right before the girl began to read. Which he had not remarked upon. It so paralysed him that he was unable to say 'Thank you' when at last she reached Gregers Werle's epoch-making words, which for him had now become the key to the play and, more, were the entrance to that clearing where the tracks he believed to have discovered were to be found and, pointing further inward, were the reasons why he had asked these lines to be read anew, because he hoped that when he got to that remark again, he would once more see this clearing and be able to follow the tracks inward. But when she got there he could not bring himself to stop her and let her go on, in her stammering fashion, to read the final, concluding exchanges in *The Wild Duck* as well. He was so vexed that he did not manage to concentrate on the play. That suppressed groan. Aggressive in all its youthful intensity. Which he had pretended not to hear. It was humiliating, although he hoped the pupils attributed his non-censure to his being so patronising that he did not bother about such trifles. But that was not the reason, as he knew in his bones. He had simply not dared to speak up, and the moment that dawned on him he had felt utterly paralysed and incapable of thinking clearly. Damn it all! He would not have dared protest against it under any circumstances, that he had to admit. And it wasn't the first time – every time the class had got to the point where one or more of them burst out in that way, giving vent to their inward righteous indignation, he gave a start and pretended not to hear it. Because he feared it. That youthful, self-righteous groan. He was afraid of what it could trigger if he rose up against it. He simply had to realise that he was afraid of them and did not dare to criticise a pupil who groaned at his teaching. He simply had to realise that he did not dare look sharply at the pupil who had taken the liberty of heaving such a bitter, heartfelt sigh at their having yet once more, in the same class hour to boot, to reread the conclusion to *The Wild Duck*, and then coldly and condescendingly reprimand him with, Save your breath, pay attention! And it was not because of cowardice; rather, he saw his fear as an expression of the shaky structures he himself represented, necessitating a certain caution on his part, not least because his young pupils, for all their arrogance, had no clear idea of the social force *they* represented. Hence he could certainly allow himself to nettle them with his exemplary teaching, but he could not provoke them so deeply that they would rise in protest and tell him they were not going to put up with it any longer. He feared the moment they would stand up, slam their desks, and demand respect for their worth, because then he would be helpless. For it was beyond doubt, after all, in view of the existing circumstances, that they were the ones who were right and he was wrong. His teaching did not measure up, because the assumptions he started from did not apply to them, and it was only a question of time, he feared, until it would be equally clear to everyone that his mission, already today quite painful, would be made superfluous. But he allowed himself nevertheless to feel an intense unease at the fact that this was the case. He let the irritation rise to his head and paralyse his tongue at the least reminder of the real state of affairs, the source of his fear. Like now. When the eighteen-year-old girl had come to the end of her stammering reading, he merely sensed an intense irritation, knowing that he was no longer capable of pursuing the track he just minutes before thought he had discovered but found no precise language for. And so he looked at his watch and said, I'm afraid we'll have to conclude our study of *The Wild Duck* for today, I have to use the rest of the class hour for some practical announcements. Experienced as he was, he managed to spin this out so that the school bell rang at the very moment the last announcement concerning homework, paper topics etc., was made, and the pupils could close their school editions of *The Wild Duck* with a bang and throw them back into their satchels, while he himself quietly closed his book. The pupils got up from their desks and stood there at ease, tall and ungainly or broad and blustery, twenty-nine young anarchical men and women who were now leaving their isolated classroom, looking forward to the break as they passed him, directly below the podium, some already with their ears plugged into their Walkmans and snapping their fingers. He, too, stood up, feeling tired, spent, and deeply disappointed. The pupils passed by in small groups, taking no notice of him as they chatted cheerfully, representing wholesome, fearless Norwegian youth to an all but overwhelming degree, now liberated from the unnatural and antiquated rituals of a double period. Suddenly he called after them: But . . . Till next Monday. Then we will finally get to the bottom of things. Then we will understand Gregers Werle's shudderings. Those convulsive twitchings the text talks about. But they passed him without giving the least indication that they had understood what he was saying, and as for his last two remarks, they probably didn't even hear them, because by then he could only see the backs of the last pupils disappearing, so that he, he had to admit, stood utterly alone in the classroom, calling after them, though that was not exactly a reason to feel annoyed – it is, after all, just a slightly comical posture I've got myself into and which they did not even notice, he added to himself.

He entered the staff room. He had only this double class on Monday (being on a reduced schedule as the head teacher of Norwegian at the school), so his work for today was now over. He attempted a condescending smile, at life and at his own role in it, but could not bring it off. Phew, he thought, there are any number of execrable things one has to put up with in this world, God knows, trying in this way to push aside the morning's unpleasant experiences before walking through the door to where his colleagues were relaxing before their next classes. He chatted with a couple of colleagues about this and that, while noticing that the effects of yesterday's aquavit had not yet completely loosened their hold on his body and brain, and he caught himself wanting to have a beer, but for that, of course, it was far too early. He felt he had succeeded in calming down, and therefore he decided to leave the school for today, having nothing to do there any more, because he could make preparations for the day tomorrow much better at home, in his own apartment. When he reached the front door he discovered it had started to rain. Not much, just a light drizzle, but enough to make him ask himself whether he should open his umbrella, he would not get very wet during that short walk home if he didn't. But since he had taken the umbrella with him in the morning, he decided to use it anyway. He opened it, but it didn't work. He had pressed the button that would cause the umbrella to open automatically, but nothing happened. He pressed the button once more, harder, but nothing happened. Not that, too, he thought, indignant. He gave it a third try, but with no success. Then he tried to force the umbrella open with his hands, but that didn't help either; the umbrella resisted, so that he just barely managed to make it spread out, and even that cost him a great effort. Then he couldn't contain himself. He was standing in the school yard at Fagerborg Secondary School, in the break, trying to open his umbrella. But he could not do it. Hundreds of pupils at the school were standing round about, and some of them must have noticed him. Enough! He walked rapidly up to the water fountain and banged the umbrella against it in a wild fury. He struck and struck the umbrella against the fountain, felt how the metal in the shaft was beginning to give and that the ribs were breaking. Delighted, he struck and struck. Through a sort of haze he saw the pupils approaching, slowly and in profound silence, as if they were stealing towards him, and now they were standing around him in a semicircle, but at a respectful distance. He was beating the increasingly limp, cracking umbrella against the fountain in a savage fury. When he noticed that the ribs were beginning to loosen, he threw the umbrella on the ground and started jumping on it, before using his heel to try and crush the umbrella with it. Then he picked up the umbrella again and banged it once more against the fountain – the ribs were now broken and uncontrollably twisted, winding in all directions, some of them cutting into his hand and leaving little scratches in the skin where he could see the blood begin to trickle out. He was surrounded by pupils all around, lurking pupils, quiet, their eyes staring. They were staring open-mouthed, standing motionless around him, but always at a respectful distance. Several of them had lunch boxes in their hands, for it was the middle of the noon break. He could make out, as through a haze, the faces of the nearest ones and, strange to say, quite clearly. A tall blonde girl was looking at him in amazement, he noticed, as were a couple of boys from the graduating class, and their faces, which looked ridiculously astonished, made him even more furious. He stared at the tall blonde. Damn twat! he yelled. Eat your food! Fat snout! And in the same instant he grabbed the umbrella, black and smashed up, and went for them full tilt. When he reached them, they drew to one side, very quickly, allowing him to lurch along between them and continue on, through the empty, wet school yard and out of it and down Fagerborggate – free, finally free, away from them! He walked hurriedly, at a violently agitated pace that accorded with his agitated condition, and in this state of mind he now began to wail as it dawned on him what he had done.

He walked down Fagerborggate, which he had done so often, but this time he did not turn right at Jacob Aalls gate, as he always used to do, but continued on down the winding Fredensborggate, until it joined Pilestredet, and went on down Pilestredet, along Stensparken, down Norabakken towards Bislett, and although he chose this way instinctively, yet it was a clear expression of his misery, because the way he now walked did not lead home, like the road that automatically guided his steps into Jacob Aalls gate, but away, to the city centre, into the tumult down there, where he could disappear, he perhaps thought, vaguely, walking with jittery steps. But one thing was clear to him, namely, that this was the end of a twenty-five years' occupation as an official educator in the Norwegian school system. This was his ultimate downfall. He knew that now he was leaving the Fagerborg school behind him for good and that he would never teach again. He had fallen, and so irredeemably that he did not even wish to rise again, not even if they pulled him up. To go back was impossible, regardless of whether the principal and his colleagues would attempt to trivialise the incident, as a collapse that could have happened to anyone. It had not happened to just anyone, it had happened to him. Had his colleagues observed the scene? The mere thought made him go rigid. For a moment he stood completely still. Good God, he exclaimed aloud, it cannot be true! But it could be true. He knew from experience that teachers sitting convivially in the staff room were extremely alert to any impropriety taking place in the school yard, for even if they did not watch but sat and talked among themselves, they listened all the time, and if suddenly there was total silence out there instead of the steady buzz and occasional shrill voices calling, not the usual thing, laughter and such, but absolute silence, at least one of them would get up and walk over to the window to see what it could be, and then one more would come, and then a third, until the entire faculty were posted at the windows, staring out at the school yard, and there they had seen ... No, no, he interrupted himself, there is no point even thinking about it. It's the end. In any case, I have to get rid of that ill-fated umbrella, he thought, looking around in a tizzy for a rubbish bin where he could leave it. But they had not heard what he had yelled, he thought, in a moment of lightheartedness, though he dared say it would not be long before they learned about it, he added sombrely to himself. But this is a disaster, he thought in near wonder. It's a real misfortune, there is no other name for it, he went on, preoccupied. What a mess I've got myself into! he burst out furiously. I must be a real idiot. But he came by no extenuating circumstances by calling himself an idiot, for however idiotic it was it was irrevocable. It's the worst thing that could ever have happened, he exclaimed, as if he could not believe his own words for a moment. What shall become of me? he exclaimed desperately to himself. And what is going to happen to her who is my wife? Yes, how can I break it to her? That the ground has suddenly been ripped away from under our feet, and that it's all my fault. What are we going to live on, in other words? he thought. And the shame of it! he added. No, life will not ever be the same, he reflected. All jittery, he walked down the quiet Fagerborggate and the equally quiet Pilestredet; there was a small rain falling, he noticed that his spectacles were getting misted and that his hair had got wet. The asphalt was black with moisture and the leaves were brown and wet, lying bunched-up along the asphalt and on the bonnets of the cars parked on this quiet residential street. The sky was a uniform grey, and sort of muzzy, now that the rain was finally falling. However, all he noticed as he passed Stensparken was a silent drizzle only, against his hair and on his spectacles. At the bottom of Norabakken he discovered a rubbish bin where at last he managed to dispose of that ill-fated umbrella, and he perceived with surprise that his body felt it as a relief to be rid of it, as if whether he was still carrying this ragged object should make any difference. He looked at his hands, from where the blood was still trickling out, and he wiped it off. Reaching Bislett, he stopped at the traffic circle there. Where should he go? He would go through the Homansbyen neighbourhood, along the lovely Josefinegate, and up to the traffic light at the Bogstadveien, where he could either continue on Josefinegate to the Uranienborg Church and Briskeby, or he could walk down Bogstadveien to Lorry (a beer, he thought, a beer would taste very good) and then down Wergelandsveien, past the Artists' House and the house of the Association of Secondary School Teachers (no, no, not that) to the city centre, or through Slottsparken, the palace park, which is never as majestic as right now, when the leaves have fallen and the trees stand there with their naked branches silhouetted against the soggy sky, and with a strange greying light between the lowest branches and the ground – a thrilling sight. He could see himself wandering along the paths of Slottsparken down to the capital's main street, Karl Johan, or he could walk up Bogstadveien to Majorstua and the well-known restaurant the Valkyrie (Valka, he thought, but then I will have made a long detour, and it will look ridiculous, even if no-one knows, when I walk through the door). Or he could continue on down Pilestredet and end up in those swarming streets in the heart of the city. But that I wouldn't have believed if I had stood here for the first time in my life and had never been to Oslo before, he thought as he looked down Pilestredet. For it looked as though to continue down Pilestredet would land him in a dangerous blind alley which led in the end to dreary warehouses, a dumping ground for tyres and rusty jalopies down in the boggy area by the harbour, because what he saw from where he was standing was, on the left, a depressing factory building, a former brewery, and on the right a row of apartment block facades of the most seedy and run-down sort, and, furthermore, as Pilestredet was very narrow, it did not seem particularly reassuring to go on down, by contrast to walking up Thereses gate, which is a lively street, full of charm. Seen from here, from the viewpoint of someone who has gone astray, it would be natural to walk up Thereses gate, because, lured by the audacious liveliness of this street, you would think that Thereses gate was located in the densest downtown area, and you would look up the steeply climbing Thereses gate and think that, at the top of the street, the city centre would open up, with magnificent avenues, the Palace and the Parliament, the National Theatre and the Opera, a real capital for an enviable people of the wealthy Occident that has lived in affluence for almost a hundred years by now, so that when the blue tram comes up Pilestredet, enters the traffic circle at Bislett and begins slowly moving up Thereses gate, one tends to think that it comes from the bleak Oslo outskirts and is on its way to the glittering centre, whereas in reality it is the direct opposite – well, Adamstua is not exactly a bleak fringe, but it is the frontier of the central city, for beyond Adamstua rural life begins, with villas and sentimental row houses, he thought, before he suddenly became furious with himself. Was this the right moment to stand here fantasising, rather than figuring out how to let your wife know about it, he thought sarcastically, or how you can while away the time for the next fifteen years, until you will receive your first retirement cheque, he thought, in the same sarcastic way. Yes, where was he to go? Past

Bislett and on, and then up Dalsbergstien to St Hanshaugen and the famous brown restaurant, the Schrøder. (A beer, he thought, and I haven't been to the Schrøder for a long time.) He was about to cross the street, first over to the Bislett Baths and then along Bislett, when he was suddenly struck by sheer aesthetic pleasure at the sight of the Bislett Stadium on the other side of the street. It's a really handsome stadium, he thought. Art Deco. An ornament to the city. Small to be the principal stadium of a European capital, but what pleasing dimensions. And how about those remarkable acoustics, with echoes from the concrete walls when the roars of enthusiasm strike them and ricochet back, he thought, before again going rigid at the thought of what he had done. Yes, what shall we live on? he asked himself in despair. What is going to happen to her? I'm afraid she will stick at nothing and humiliate both herself and me. I will not be able to take it, he thought darkly. But if this is true, and unfortunately it is, then it is all over, he exclaimed inwardly, shaking his head so forcefully in despair at himself that the passersby gave him inquisitive glances. Standing there by the traffic circle at Bislett, as uncertain as ever which direction to take, he looked in perplexity at his hands, which were still blood-stained, and got out his handkerchief, holding it over the deepish cut that was still bleeding.

So it is his wife Elias Rukla is worried about, now that he has got himself into this painful position, which means that he must say goodbye to his entire social existence; it was impossible to conceive of any other conclusion to the avalanche that had overwhelmed him, and even if he could, it would not have changed anything, since he would simply have shrugged his shoulders at every other proposed solution and uttered a stubborn 'no'. Her name is Eva Linde, and when Elias Rukla met her she was decidedly attractive, as she also was when he married her eight years later. That eight years went by from when he met her until she became his wife was due to the fact that, in the meantime, she had been married to his best friend. That was how he met her. As Johan Corneliussen's woman. This was at the end of the 1960s, and they were all three in their twenties, with Elias Rukla approaching thirty, the two other, the sweethearts, coming up for twenty-four.

Elias Rukla had made the acquaintance of Johan Corneliussen in the Institute of Philosophy at the University of Oslo, Blindern – in 1966, it must have been. He happened to be there to fulfil the requirements for his university degree in language and literature, while at the same time preparing his thesis in Norwegian literature; by that time he had completed two minors, in Norwegian and history respectively, and he was still wavering between history and Norwegian as his major subject, continuing to do so even after he had begun to prepare his thesis in Norwegian, and therefore it suited him to choose elementary level philosophy as the third subject he needed in any case at that point. At the institute he met Johan Corneliussen, who was already then firmly set on taking a PhD in philosophy, and for some reason they became good friends, so good, in fact, that during certain periods they were practically inseparable, as they say, and, as far as friendships between students go, often quite correctly. They were extremely different, both in temperament and, not least, as far as sociability or social gifts were concerned, so their friendship might have struck others as rather peculiar, if it had not been for the fact that close friendships between young people of the same gender do tend to be peculiar.

Elias Rukla first noticed Johan Corneliussen at a lecture in a course on Wittgenstein which the two of them, both the elementary student and the PhD candidate, attended, something that ought to have made Elias Rukla understand that he had probably bitten off more than he could chew. Near the end of the lecture, Johan Corneliussen had posed a question, and the lecturer, a noted Wittgenstein disciple, had taken it very seriously. To Elias Rukla the question had appeared quite ordinary, having to do with a distinction between two concepts which, to him, had seemed quite simple, but the lecturer looked greatly taken aback and stood absolutely still for at least two minutes before he turned to the student who had asked the question and talked directly to him, both for the rest of the hour and longer, until a new group of students streamed into the seminar room for another lecture. This made Elias Rukla conclude that the student questioner was not just anybody, which proved to be the case. It was whispered at the Institute of Philosophy that he had a great future ahead of him. The publication of his PhD dissertation on Immanuel Kant would be a real event. Later, Elias Rukla often saw him strolling through the corridors on the ninth floor of Niels Treschow's

House at Blindern, where the Institute of Philosophy was located, and he would think, There goes a man my own age who will perhaps some day be known as a great philosopher. One day he saw him engaged in discussion in the middle of a flock of students. Elias Rukla noticed how he was basking in the lustre of his fellow students, not least the females among them. They paid attention to his arguments, and they obviously liked to be close to him and listen to what he said. Not only what he said, but also the voice in which he said it. They were in the middle of a discussion, and Elias Rukla noticed that when Johan Corneliussen had finished speaking and another student had the floor, either to add to what Johan Corneliussen had said or to contradict him, they were still looking at Johan Corneliussen. They were waiting for him to answer, looking forward to it with expectation, in fact, especially the female students. And it looked as though he enjoyed it, Elias Rukla thought, and to his amazement he noticed that he had not meant it to be a disparaging observation. He liked the self-satisfied and happy air of Johan Corneliussen as he stood there at the centre of a group of debating students. There was a sense of openness and vitality about it. Elias Rukla was sitting on a bench by himself, well outside the circle of the eagerly debating students, so he could not hear what it was all about, only that they were discussing, and he caught himself wishing he'd been part of this circle, however unnatural that seemed to him, since, after all, he was only a beginner in the subject, with nothing to contribute, and though he could have joined the circle as an interested listener, he felt that even that would appear obtrusive. But when a bit later, after the group had broken up, Johan Corneliussen walked past together with two other students, he caught himself envying them, because already now it seemed to Elias Rukla that to be on speaking terms with Johan Corneliussen would enrich one's life. So when Elias Rukla a few days later was again sitting on this bench as Johan Corneliussen came down the corridor by himself and then flopped down on the same bench, Elias Rukla grew rigid with shyness. May I cadge a smoke from you? Johan Corneliussen asked. Elias Rukla nodded and handed him his tobacco pouch. Johan Corneliussen rolled a cigarette from Elias Rukla's pouch and handed it back to him with a friendly nod. Then they went on sitting next to one another, Johan Corneliussen smoking. Neither of them said anything. Finally Elias asked, Why are you studying philosophy?

Johan Corneliussen scrutinised Elias Rukla, quickly and closely, but since he could not perceive any sign of laughter, either in his face or in his voice, he replied, And you? Why are you studying philosophy? To that, Elias Rukla replied, I'm only taking an elementary course. I need to straighten out my head before I get going on my thesis in Norwegian. My brain is deficient in order. — Hm, to learn a sense of order, well, I never! I never heard the likes. What are you writing your thesis on? Ibsen? — Yes, Elias Rukla replied, I've thought about it. —Haven't I seen you in Jacob's Wittgenstein seminar? —Yes, Elias replied, while noting that Johan Corneliussen used the first name of the famous Wittgenstein disciple who was in charge of the seminar and that it sounded natural coming from him. Johan Corneliussen evidently found the juxtaposition of Ibsen and Wittgenstein interesting, for he proposed that they go to Frederikke (the students' canteen, bar, restaurant, dining room) to have a beer. They did, sat talking together for several hours over one beer after another, and when it was beginning to get dark, Johan Corneliussen proposed that they go to Jordal Amphitheatre to see VIC against GIC.

Through the city in the waning March light. Patches of ice and slush. A drizzly evening as they got off the tram and changed to a bus. The March wind and the desolate blocks of apartment houses. Then Jordal Amphitheatre. An ice-hockey stadium in Oslo's East End. Floodlights. Johan Corneliussen and Elias Rukla watching from the terraces, together with three to four hundred other ice-hockey enthusiasts (Elias Rukla was not one). That grey, matte sheet of ice. Bundled-up players in helmets and leggings, hunched over and balancing on the ice in their short hockey skates and their colourful get-ups. The sticks. The black, flat puck (which is so difficult to follow, Elias Rukla thought). The sound of the runners against the ice. The sound of a fall as the players collide. The sound of the sticks against the ice. They found themselves in the middle of the GIC camp, which was the smaller. GIC, or Gamlebyen, was the ice-hockey club of those who lived in the Gamlebyen section of downtown Oslo. It was a venerable old club, but in decline. VIC, or Vålerenga, was the club of those who lived in the Vålerenga section, a little further north and east. Gamlebyen was on its last legs, while Vålerenga would have many brilliant years before it. Johan Corneliussen, who was not from Oslo but had come here from a railway town in the East Country, was therefore rooting for GIC. There he stood, together with Elias Rukla, cheering from the terraces. Taking out a small hip-flask, he offered Elias a nip, took one himself and passed the flask around. I like hockey better than football, he told Elias afterwards, but you mustn't tell that to a soul, do you hear? You hear? Elias asked why he liked hockey better than football (with Elias it was the direct opposite). Quite simple. Rhythm, said Johan Corneliussen. The rhythm of hockey suits us better. —Us? Elias said. —Yes, us, Johan Corneliussen replied, unruffled, people of the 1960s. Hockey is sport's answer to rock'n'roll. They were then sitting at the Stortorvet Inn, drinking more beer. They sat there till it closed, and afterwards they set out for the student village at Sogn, where they both lived, though in widely different parts, but they did not trek up there in order to turn in, in their several quarters, but to go to a party. Johan Corneliussen knew of an apartment where there was a party, and that was where they wanted to go. They rang the bell, Johan Corneliussen was welcomed by radiant faces, and they immediately mingled with the company. One beer after another. Well into the night, Elias Rukla discovered that Johan Corneliussen disappeared into a room with a woman; a little later he went to sleep at the table of the large communal kitchen that belonged to the apartment where the party was given. He was sleeping with his hands cupped around his head, at first hearing some sounds around him but then nothing.

He felt someone touching his shoulder. He looked up, and there was Johan Corneliussen. The light barely filtered through the windows of this kitchen at the Sogn student village. In his hands, Johan Corneliussen was holding a bottle of frosty aquavit. Breakfast, he proclaimed. He began taking sandwich spread out of the refrigerator, herring, cheese. Boiled eggs. Elias Rukla went to the bathroom and splashed his mug with some water. The first batch of the students living there came crawling out of their rooms. They had all been at the party the evening before and were now offered breakfast. They sat down at the large kitchen table, men and women all mixed up, and some even let themselves be forced to sample the ice-cold aquavit and take a glass of beer, managing thereby to kill a day of study, while others said a firm no and were thus able to drag themselves down to Blindern. Among those who sat down at the breakfast table was the female student Elias Rukla thought Johan Corneliussen had disappeared into a room with during the night, just eating her breakfast, saying no to anything to drink. She was sitting beside Johan Corneliussen, but nothing suggested there was anything between them, or that there had been anything between them last night, for that matter. Johan Corneliussen spoke to her in a friendly way, on the merry side, marked by his hangover and now once more by rising intoxication, rising like the March sun outside, rising golden against the windows here at the Sogn student village, and she laughed with him as though she had not been together with him that night, or rather as though she *had* been together with him that night, but now it was morning, with the sun shining for a new day, which for her meant study at Blindern, for Johan a new day of increasing intoxication, which would suddenly die down in the late afternoon, leaving, one had to assume, a severe fatigue. But that was far away in the future. Right now they were sitting in a kitchen at the Sogn student village, Johan Corneliussen, Elias Rukla, and two more students, one male and one female, drinking aquavit and beer, but when the clock passed twelve, Johan Corneliussen began to get restless. Wanting to go on, he asked Elias Rukla if he would come along. They rushed out into the broad daylight, down the hills at the Sogn student village, towards fresh experiences. Johan had a bottle of aquavit, which was now half empty, not to say half full, in his inside pocket as they stumped down the hills to the city. Yes, it was one long, long hill all along down to Oslo's city centre, and they staggered and stumped and fell and skidded down. At the bottom of the hill was a big city, the capital of a small country called Norway, as both of them knew, for their linguistic knowledge was immense, so they could tell right away what language was spoken by the natives who crowded in upon them from every direction. Indeed, they knew quite simply from the pitch, the fact that the natives' voices rose so high at the end of a sentence, so as experts they could look at each other and proclaim in unison: It's *Norwegian*, we are in Norway. Yes, they were in Norway, the capital of Norway with its Palace and Grotto, Parliament and Administration, Enevold Falsen, Frederik the Sixth, University, National Theatre, neon signs, department stores and flag-draped streets. Yes, flags were flying on Karl Johans gate, flags and banners randomly displayed, look, the Norwegian flag and the German flag, no, it's a Belgian flag – anyway, they were hanging side by side all along the festive street; hearing shouts of hurrah and seeing a crowd of people waving their own flags at two black limousines coming down the bumpy Karl Johans gate, Johan Corneliussen and Elias Rukla, rather dazed, swerved into a side-street, and the side-street ran crosswise and was, very significantly, called Grensen, the Border. Yes, they had reached Grensen, and there came a blue tram, too, right enough, and off they ran after it and got the door smack in the face (Johan), so that he quite simply saw a sun and myriads of stars (as he told Elias, who stood bent over him, helping him up again), while the tram had stopped and the driver come running up, and now, NOW, Johan Corneliussen, having been helped to his feet again by Elias and standing upright, his coat open, succeeded in negotiating with the driver, making him actually go into the steering box and open the doors wide for them so they could triumphantly enter the promised car, which carried them through the downtown area before it once again began to rise, still with gloomy apartment blocks on both sides, and then they were suddenly in a built-up suburban area, and after an endless journey through this area the tram stopped altogether, at an end station, the driver left his car and Johan and Elias along with him. They had a long, instructive conversation with the driver, who was an expert on rock formations, varieties of stone, and volcanic deposits in the area within a radius of sixty miles, with this point as the centre of a circle. But when the tram was to start down again, with the same driver at the wheel, they said goodbye to their dear friend and set out on their own along the local roads, lined with private residences. And then, worse luck, they lost their way! The houses were so alike, all the roads about equally wide, and the snowbanks thrown up by the plough were everywhere of the same form and height, and since not a soul was to be seen, they were all at sea in the labyrinth where they found themselves. They walked for hours trying to find their way out but with no success, not until the late afternoon when the men came home from work in their cars, then they managed to stop one of these returning men after he had garaged his car and was running up to his well-protected residence at the end of a very nicely cleared path twenty metres away, and to get this somewhat distrustful man to explain to them how to solve the problem of getting back to the tramcar stop. It was high time, because in just an hour the downhill race in St Anton would be on television, Johan Corneliussen said. But they made it. They stormed into Krølle, which was Johan Corneliussen's favourite restaurant at the time, five minutes before the downhill race started. This basement restaurant had a TV. It was enthroned on top of a cabinet on the wall. They sat down at one of the tables for two, Johan in such a way that he could look straight at the TV set, Elias directly across from him, so that he had to turn around to look at the same TV. The downhill race in St Anton. One after another they turned up on the screen, in helmets and Alpine gear, before they threw themselves down the mountainsides of (or among) the Alps. Heini Messner, Austria. Jean-Claude Killy, France. Franz Vogler, West Germany. Leo Lacroix, France. Martin Heidegger, Germany. Edmund Husserl, Germany. Elias Canetti, Romania. Allen Ginsberg, USA. William Burroughs, USA. Antonio Gramsci, Italy. Jean-Paul Sartre, France. Ludwig Wittgenstein, Austria. Johan Corneliussen knew the strengths and weaknesses of all the racers and continually informed Elias that now, now, he had to watch out, for there, on that slope, Jean-Paul Sartre will have some problems, whereas now, just look how Ludwig Wittgenstein's suppleness manifests itself in that long flat stretch, and look how the Romanian Canetti saves tenths of seconds by shortening that turn, almost as nicely as the Frenchman Jean-Claude Killy. After the race they felt a creeping weariness, and they began to nod over their empty beer glasses as hunger gnawed at them. They had no money. But Johan Corneliussen knew a remedy. He beckoned to the waitress and explained the embarrassing situation that he, a regular customer, and his good friend, Elias Rukla over there, had ended up in, and shortly there appeared two glasses of beer and two plates crammed with hamburgers, onions, potatoes and peas and carrots, while a cruet stand with different spices and sauces was brought to their table, among which you could recognise black HP sauce, yellow vinaigrette, red ketchup, and mustard. They ate. Drank and ate. And took a nip or two from the bottle, while observing absolute discretion. They conversed profoundly about films they had seen. About the white over-exposed light on the women in *Last Year in Marienbad*, and the white over-exposed light on the deserted coffee tables at daybreak in Fellini's *8½*. Johan Corneliussen began to talk about the man from Kongsberg, who had in many ways cast long shadows upon his youthful life. It took a while before Elias understood he was talking about Immanuel Kant and that Kongsberg was obviously a translation of Königsberg. The man from Kaliningrad, Elias retorted, when he got it. Johan Corneliussen expressed his great love of simple sentences, which said no more than they said and where the first segment was identical with the last, and of the revelation he sometimes experienced when time and place panned out in such a way that it was possible to pronounce, with the greatest inevitability and beauty, a sentence such as an open door is an open door. They sat like this for several hours, but then Johan Corneliussen became restless and said they should go to another party. In the student village at Sogn once again. A different party this time, in a different apartment and a different building, with new prizes, as Johan Corneliussen said. They travelled up there, rang the doorbell, and Johan Corneliussen was beamingly welcomed by the one who opened. They blended into the warmth and the music. The apartment was full of students, all with glasses and bottles in their hands. Elias tried to stay close to Johan Corneliussen, but he slipped up and lost sight of him. Instead he found himself with a glass in his hand, as well as a bottle, from which accordingly he filled up the glass he had in his hand, even as also the bottle, which he had in his hand, the other hand, to be sure. Did you ever see the like! Two hands, each hand occupied with its own thing! The party moved past him without interruption, it was almost too much of a good thing, and Johan Corneliussen also moved past him and disappeared again, turned up and disappeared, together with so much else that also turned up and disappeared. Dark-haired girls from Sunnmøre and interior Sogn, fair-haired ones from Trysil, altogether far too much of everything. He tries to call out to the jamboree – after all, he's also there, but somehow he cannot get in contact with anyone. Forsaken, forsaken. Where is Johan Corneliussen? Why isn't someone talking to him, even though he calls out to them? When he woke up it was quiet. And dark. He had again woken up at the kitchen table of an apartment in the student village at Sogn. Someone had been kind enough to turn off the light so it was dark in the kitchen. But through the darkness there gleamed a small, faint glimmer of light coming from outside, and he understood that the night was coming to an end and that it was the weak early grey light of a new morning in the month of March he was now witnessing. By his side he could make out Johan Corneliussen, who was also sleeping there. He lay with his head smack on the table, snoring. It was completely quiet, apart from the fact that Johan Corneliussen was snoring, his mouth open. Elias Rukla was now utterly worn out. He realised that, for him, the party was over. He was black with wear and tear in his whole body. Still, he was glad that Johan Corneliussen, too, had settled down. He understood he had found a true friend. He nudged him, causing Johan Corneliussen to start up, awake. —I'm going now. Are you? Johan nodded, then collapsed again; his head fell on the table and he slept. Elias nudged him again. —Listen, should we go? Johan nodded and got up, abruptly and elaborately. They went into the hallway, retrieved their overcoats and put them on. They walked out into the early dawn and, their worn-out bodies cold and shivery, went down to a crossroads, where their ways parted. —We'll meet again, Johan said. —Yes, Elias said.

And they did. Elias Rukla became Johan Corneliussen's friend; they were constantly together and could be seen everywhere in each other's company. Even after Elias was done with his basic philosophy and went back to his Norwegian major, which, for that matter, he had not entirely abandoned, having retained his seat in the reading room at the Nordic Institute even while he was studying for his philosophy exam. There is no denying that Elias Rukla admired his friend. True, he tried to hide this from his friend, as well as from others, but whether he succeeded is an open question. However, he did not hide it from himself. He was clearly aware that he admired his inseparable friend and that, to tell the truth, he was proud to be constantly near him, so near, in fact, that when the others caught sight of Elias, they looked around to see whether Johan Corneliussen was not there as well. He was also aware that when Johan Corneliussen appeared, the others also counted on him, Elias, being in the vicinity and glanced briefly sideways to confirm this as a fact, as part of the very phenomenon that was Johan Corneliussen. This flattered him, even though he fully realised that, to the others, he was a person who lived in the shadow of Johan Corneliussen. But anyway, since it pointed to the obvious fact that Elias Rukla was Johan Corneliussen's friend, it had to mean that there must be something about him, too, in the eyes of the others. Elias Rukla himself often wondered what it could be. There must be something about him that caused Johan Corneliussen to prefer his company to that of others, who were seemingly both more witty, amusing and extrovert, and also more open vis-à-vis Johan Corneliussen than he was. But what that could be was a riddle to him, and he had better not worry too much about what it could be, he thought – for if I discovered what it was it would either disappear or change into its unsympathetic opposite, insofar as I then would show it in a completely different way than I do now when I do not know what it is, or it will turn out to be something inferior, something that shows both Johan and me in a not very flattering light, as, for example, the fact that what Johan likes about me is that I try as well as I can to hide how much I admire him, Elias thought. But the mere fact of his thinking this way made him feel embarrassed, and when this embarrassment came over him particularly when he was with his friend Johan Corneliussen, he would occasionally be extremely sullen, even though Johan Corneliussen might be bubbling over with high spirits, and at such times, they must have been an odd pair of friends: the cheerful, life-affirming Johan Corneliussen in the company of his sullen, grumpy shadow. But his sullenness was, of course, only due to his trying to hide that he was overwhelmed with gratitude because Johan Corneliussen was his friend and to his having such warm feelings for him that he felt shy and miserable when this warmth swept through him, flowing towards his friend on the other side of, say, the coffee table.

His friendship with Johan Corneliussen was enriching him. Johan Corneliussen's appetite for life was enormous and caused the two of them to lead a very good but hectic life as students. With study, parties and discussion, and an aimless chase after life and happiness. Johan Corneliussen was so versatile in his interests, and moved so effortlessly among them, that Elias Rukla, who followed him for the most part, had never before had such an intense feeling of being alive. Johan Corneliussen moved without difficulty from ice hockey to Kant, from interest in advertising posters to the Frankfurt school of philosophy, from rock'n'roll to classical music. Operettas and Arne Nordheim. He would throw himself into it, his brain spinning feverishly, and he would analyse and whoop simultaneously, in one and the same moment. Music, ice hockey, literature, film, football, advertising, politics, skating. Plus downhill skiing, in which he took a special interest. Second-hand bookshops and Bislett. Film clubs and TV sets. Essentially he was a spectator. He did not go in for sports very much himself, but he was hungry for sports as a spectator. He was happy in the terraces at Bislett, and most of all in Jordal Amphitheatre, among the diminishing band of Gamlebyen fans, and in front of the TV set when the great downhill races in the Alps came into our living rooms up here in the extreme North. For Johan Corneliussen, living room in this case invariably meant Krølle, the basement restaurant in the immediate vicinity of the Uranienborg Church where he and Elias were very often to be found at the same table for two for several years to come, seated in the same position as the first time they met, Johan with his face turned towards the telly up on the wall, Elias with his back to it, half turned, so that he partly watched the skiers set off down the hill, partly listened to Johan Corneliussen's expert and confident commentary. It was not the fact that Johan Corneliussen was interested both in philosophy and sports which fascinated Elias Rukla, because that was true of many, not least Elias himself. It was that he did not grade his interests, either emotionally or intellectually. He was equally enthusiastic about a well-executed downhill race as about a well-made film by Jean-Luc Godard and plunged into both with equally great analytical passion.

With Elias Rukla he discussed philosophy very little, and only when Elias was looking for some useful tips about his approaching examination in basic philosophy. He was reluctant to talk about Immanuel Kant. But Elias Rukla knew with what sense of expectancy his PhD degree (which was a thing of the remote future) was awaited. Hence Elias Rukla thought (often) that there was something incomprehensible about him. He felt that Johan Corneliussen was wasting his time by being so much together with him, doing so many things outside his field of study and, not least, expending so much energy and enthusiasm on what he did. He often had to admit that he could not understand his appetite for life. What had made a young man with such hunger for life throw himself into the study of philosophy? Do those with the greatest zest for life often choose to study philosophy? If that is so, why do the ones with the greatest hunger for life choose human *thought* as their field? Instead of, say, studying to be engineers? When Elias Rukla thought about this, it struck him that those of his classmates from secondary school who had begun to study engineering were not noted for any exceptional zest for life, even though they had chosen a profession which would set them up for becoming men of action. They were the ones who would construct and build, get the wheels to roll and the machines to run, and make the people under them obey their orders, because unless they were obeyed, the wheels would not turn, the machines not run, and the buildings not be built, one might say. But on reflection, Elias found that the classmates who had now become engineers possessed no particular appetite for life at all, they were merely good in school, but essentially quite unimaginative, well, quite conformist, and that was true about all of them, without exception, Elias thought. The only trace of imagination he had discovered among these would-be engineers was a general predilection for telling jokes and singing songs from the student revues in Trondheim. But Johan Corneliussen neither told jokes nor sang ditties from student revues. He was simply stuck on life. And he had plunged into a demanding study of the great philosopher Immanuel Kant, and the brief reports he had leaked to teachers and fellow students about his discoveries had aroused their highest expectations. This (still) young man, who wanted to take in everything, who did not let a party in the student village at Sogn that he knew of take place without at least dropping by, if only for a few minutes, to see what was going on, whether he was missing out on anything, and who, if he was missing out on something, could even so go back to his room to review a certain Kant interpretation, because then he knew at least *what* he was missing, what possibilities were lying in wait for this night, as befitted someone who, in other words, was extremely curious and was known for his great flair for gossip among his associates in the student milieu at Blindern and Sogn – this (still) young man, who would have an attack of panic because he was afraid to miss, due to other business, an important home match of Skeid (which was his team, not Vålerenga) or, for that matter, an absurd play presented by the Television Theatre, and who, on learning that Molde was organizing an annual jazz festival, with a line-up of international big guns in the bright light of summer, planned to go there, which he did (with a tent and all, but without Elias Rukla for his travelling companion, unlike their three big drunken binges for the sheer adventure of it in Copenhagen, going by the Danish line, where they slept on deck), this young man had as the basis of his life, the fixed point of his existence, the eighteenth-century thinker Immanuel Kant from the East-Prussian city of Königsberg on the Baltic. Elias Rukla never ceased to wonder about it. Behind that forehead of his he lives a quiet, contemplative life, he thought, something I simply cannot comprehend. And so he quizzed and quizzed Johan Corneliussen about his contemplative life with Immanuel Kant. Johan disliked being quizzed in this way and would get annoyed at times, but Elias Rukla did not give a tinker's damn about that. He asked and asked, but Johan Corneliussen preferred to talk about something else, something that was going to happen, perhaps even the same evening. But now and then Johan Corneliussen did speak about what his life was based upon. Then Elias would prick up his ears, although he had to admit he did not grasp very much. After all, his knowledge of Immanuel Kant did not go beyond what an elementary student of philosophy had to know, and to grasp even that had cost him hard work. But he pricked up his ears. In any case, he understood that Johan Corneliussen was bound up with Time and Space, these two categories which are there, by necessity, in every thought we think. Here everything bumps up against its limit. Time. Space. That which was given in advance, and which Johan Corneliussen's brain was pulling and tearing at, Elias Rukla presumed. Would not someone who could relate to this without cracking up possess an inward composure, display an air of being transfigured? Elias Rukla looked expectantly at Johan Corneliussen, his cheerful and generous friend. But Johan Corneliussen gave no answer to this. He kept his eventual meditations, as well as his eventual transfiguration, his priceless and possibly hard-earned inward composure, to himself. But he said that it was not Kant per se that interested him. Kant was the basis, but that was not what he was after in his PhD dissertation, which was still several years in the future. He was occupied by all the others, all those thousands of philosophers who had taken up a position towards Kant. It was the Kant literature, the literature *about* Kant. It was modern man's dossier. By studying that, one was truly studying the possibilities of human thought. There was no need to study anything else. The literature about Kant contained everything that a curious and intelligent twentieth-century individual could imagine himself asking questions about. By means of Marx's relation to Kant, you learned everything. That way alone you would be able to understand Marxism. The same with Wittgenstein. Studying how Wittgenstein works with Kant, how, with all due respect, he tries to evade him, you are immediately on the track of Wittgenstein's secret. He himself was trying to join that numerous celebrated company – well, the end he had in view was that his PhD dissertation would in the fullness of time join this series of dossiers of human thought. But that was, of course, such a high aim that he was reluctant to talk aloud about it, he wasn't a megalomaniac and was loath to be considered pretentious, being, after all, simply a twenty-eight-year-old from a railway town in East Norway, and he certainly had not *seen* the truth, in case someone should get that idea, but he was trying to come up with a few modest possibilities within this great continuous tradition constituted by two hundred years of humble and passionate interpretation of Kant. However, to get it right he had to take his time over it. Hence the slow pace of his studies. So slow that at the time he met Eva Linde he had already been studying philosophy for eight years, and even so he was far, far away from seeing the end of his study for the PhD.

By that time, however, Elias Rukla had seen the end of *his* study. In the autumn of 1968 he obtained his university degree in the humanities, and in the spring of 1969 he took the so-called pedagogical seminar, to prepare himself for a career in secondary school, the *gymnasium*. He moved from the student village at Sogn, having found a relatively reasonable three-room apartment in Jacob Aalls gate, took out a bank loan and bought it, even though he had not yet acquired a livelihood. That he did, however, in the course of the spring, at the Fagerborg school, where he was to start teaching in the autumn as a fully trained senior master, with the pedagogical seminar and all behind him. Johan Corneliussen went on as before, as a student admired by his fellow students of both genders. Now he was even a student leader, for a spirit of revolt was sweeping through the European universities at the time, and that turned Johan Corneliussen into a declared Marxist; but since Marx depends on Kant, as we have seen, it did not have any momentous consequences for Johan Corneliussen's studies. He continued as before. He and Elias still stuck together, through thick and thin. Elias often visited Johan in the student village, and from there they set out on expeditions into the real world. Only one thing was changed, namely, that Johan Corneliussen suddenly insisted on introducing to Elias Rukla a young lady he had met. This was something new, for previously Johan Corneliussen had always kept the ladies 'apart' from their friendship. He had constantly 'hooked up' with women on their joint journeys through life's labyrinths, and at student parties, and more than once he had even 'dated' one and the same young woman for several weeks, most often a fellow student he had captured, or let himself be captured by, and with whom he let himself be seen in the student canteen or other places, but without making much of it; he would rush straight up to Elias with his young lady in tow and settle down without any fuss, as if all three of them were old friends, and after a few weeks she was usually gone and he referred to her quite naturally as a good friend whom neither of them saw so often any more. But then one day he invited Elias for dinner in his little apartment in the Sogn student village, because he would like him to meet a young woman he had come to know.

When he arrived at the student village they were waiting for him. On the sofa of Johan Corneliussen's cramped little apartment. The table was spruced up with a white tablecloth, set with plates and glasses, and with a paper napkin at each place setting. A festive mood. When Elias Rukla saw Eva Linde for the first time. When Elias Rukla stepped into the small room where Johan Corneliussen lived and slept, in order to testify to what he would now witness: the couple on the sofa. She stood up from where she sat beside Johan Corneliussen, and took Elias Rukla's hand, and he noticed that she gave his hand a warm (possibly imploring) 'extra' shake. The new couple seemed anxious, Johan Corneliussen nevertheless expectant. And so he had every reason to be. The beauty of the young lady was such as to have an air of unreality about it. To be in the same room with her, and in such a small room, a virtual ship's cabin, was a strange experience. He hoped she would go into the kitchen to prepare the meal and serve it. But that was done by Johan, who vanished in order to serve the dinner. Everything had been prepared in advance, so he was not away for very long. But for this short while he was alone with her. Swallowing, he asked her what she was doing. She said she was taking her prelims at the university. Yes, of course, Elias Rukla said, I should have thought of that. She smiled, ostensibly not the least bit surprised by the rather silly exclamation of Elias Rukla. She probably had the same thought as he, namely that Elias Rukla had put two and two together and figured out that she was Johan Corneliussen's pupil. As a gifted PhD student in philosophy, he had already for several years had a welcome extra income from preparing students for their preliminary examination in philosophy. 'Stud. Mag. Art. Johan Corneliussen reviews special logical approaches to problems', it said in the course catalogue, where his name was listed among university lecturers and professors. She had not looked him straight in the face when she smiled, but smiled discreetly sideways, towards the window. Of course, because Johan was not in the room, Elias had thought. He liked her because of that. Johan entered with the food. Beefsteak in Béarnaise sauce, which Johan had made himself. From the ground up. Red wine, Beaujolais Thorin. This was the first (and only) time Elias was invited to dinner in Johan Corneliussen's apartment. They drank a toast, and the indescribably beautiful Eva Linde also raised her glass and drank to Elias, a bit constrainedly, and afterwards to Johan, but then so close, so close. The meal. It was a meal to which Johan Corneliussen had invited him. The indescribably beautiful Eva Linde ate almost invisibly, and so quietly that Elias nearly had to hold his breath and scarcely dared to swallow, for fear that a sound might then escape from his own mouth, not to mention the soundless concentration with which he chewed so as not to give the least offence vis-à-vis the quiet beauty sitting on the sofa beside Johan Corneliussen, as his chosen mate. No doubt sensing the clammy silence in the room during the meal, Johan Corneliussen began to talk, but it was not to her, his chosen Eva, that he talked, in order to make her visible, but to him, the friend. He began to converse with his friend, taking as his point of departure the things they usually talked about. Accordingly, Elias understood he should act exactly as before and behave towards him, Johan, as though Eva were not present. They were to talk together as they had always talked together. Elated, Johan Corneliussen opened the conversation, speaking insistently, imploringly. Be natural, Elias! Do not bother to entertain Eva Linde, talk to me, your friend Johan! Everything was to be as before, Elias understood Johan was trying to tell him, the only new thing was that Eva, with her lovely, delicate nature, would be present. And they talked, the two old friends, about things they had talked about thousands of times before, as Eva Linde sat quietly listening.

That was how the evening went. The two friends talked together about politics, mutual friends (gossip), sports results, countries and kingdoms, about where the future came from, in which shape it would come and what message it would bring etc., etc. Johan Corneliussen elated and enthusiastic (not least now, as a rebellious Marxist), Elias more sceptical, even a bit pedestrian now and then, at best displaying a dry sense of humour (he hoped). As so many times before. Johan in the sofa, Elias in the lone armchair. But beside Johan in the sofa, Eva Linde, the chosen mate. From time to time, when Elias put in a dryly humorous remark (which was his trademark), a little smile flitted across her indescribably beautiful face, and then Elias found it difficult to pretend he was not affected by this modest positive reaction from this incredibly attractive woman. He had never been in the same room with such an attractive woman before! In some way he felt like an intruder, and as the hours went by he several times made as if to get up and take his leave, so the loving pair could be by themselves, as was meet and proper. But Johan Corneliussen urged him to stay. And so Elias Rukla stayed, for, after all, he could not say, which was perfectly true, that out of consideration for Eva Linde, who was no doubt eager to be alone with Johan now, doubtless tired of having to sit all evening doing nothing but listening, and who was probably looking forward to only one thing, to be alone with him at last, that he, Elias, was taking up her time and, out of consideration for her, would leave – that he could not say, it would not be very courteous towards her. And besides, Eva Linde seemed to be enjoying herself. Seeing that the two friends went on talking, she sort of settled down. She eventually kicked off her shoes and curled up on the sofa. She did not lean against Johan, though she kept sitting beside him, but the glances she sent him, the way she looked at him, the way she smiled at him, were such that Elias Rukla had to lower his eyes, moved by the very possibility of bestowing such glances on a common mortal. And once she patted the sleeve of Johan Corneliussen's jacket, brushing away a bit of dust, from a cigarette or the like, and that movement made Elias Rukla understand that the almost incredibly attractive Eva Linde had lost her heart to Johan Corneliussen, and again he had to look away, dazzled by the solemn nature of that reality.

Only after midnight did Johan Corneliussen accept Elias Rukla's desire to withdraw, leaving the loving couple to themselves. Getting up from his armchair, he remarked on the lateness of the hour and said he had to turn out early the next morning, also that he had better not drink any more wine tonight. Johan Corneliussen and Eva got up too, from the sofa, and walked him out into the common hallway. Johan and Elias exchanged a few jovial private words, incomprehensible to anyone else, and Eva Linde gave him her hand for goodbye. A firm handshake, but without that 'extra' (imploring) pressure she had applied to his hand when they greeted one another for the first time a few hours earlier. He was pleased that she did it that way. A little later he was strolling down Sognsveien, away from the student village to his own apartment in Jacob Aalls gate. He was all wistfulness, reflecting that youth was irretrievably over and that it was about time for him to think of settling down. He felt lonely, although Johan Corneliussen had throughout shown him great generosity in the midst of his happiness and had indirectly used the entire evening to tell him, well, assure him, and her, that their friendship was so precious to him that not even love and its object would get in its way; quite the contrary, Johan Corneliussen had said, it was the object of his love who had to be worked into the friendship. This all-but-stuttering highminded-ness on the part of Johan Corneliussen moved him profoundly, but he knew that it was based on a wish rather than reality, because with a woman like Eva Linde as the object of his love, he, Elias Rukla, also understood that cultivating her would swallow all his time, for Johan Corneliussen must be all ablaze now, burning with the fire of a passion that threatened to consume him unless he was continually near the one who fed this fire, so he could see her and be intimate with her, Elias Rukla thought.

He was deeply moved by Johan Corneliussen's indirect assurances, however unrealistic, vis-à-vis himself, and he felt he owed him something in return. Hence he could get no peace until (after many tries) he managed to get hold of Johan Corneliussen on the telephone the next day. He had been calling him all day on the communal telephone, which he knew was located in the hallway in the group of apartment buildings where he lived in the Sogn student village, but the person who picked up the telephone had told him every time, after Elias had heard him knock on Johan Corneliussen's door, that he was not home. Only in the early evening did he succeed in reaching him. Then he said, without introduction, What a wonderful woman. I envy you, take good care of her. I think you should marry her. Johan Corneliussen was silent. Then Elias heard him give a laugh, a rather embarrassed laugh, but embarrassed because he was glad. —You don't say, you don't say. Huh-huh. — Well, that was all. Cheerio. —Yes, cheerio. Elias hung up.

Now several months went by before he again heard from Johan Corneliussen. When he telephoned, early in the autumn, it was to invite Elias to join in a group project. A three-room apartment at Grorud was to be renovated. He turned up at the appointed time and place, together with ten or twelve others of Johan's friends. It was a small apartment, cramped and run-down. Johan Corneliussen's friends renovated it. They plastered and painted, hung wallpaper and put down flooring. Heaps of materials were delivered, always by some private person who had obviously arranged something for Johan. Johan Corneliussen himself was at the centre of the project, organising the whole thing. He snapped his fingers, and up rose a bright, attractive, modern three-room flat in this tower block at Grorud in no time at all. And here Eva Linde was to move in. She did not know anything yet, he was to meet her downtown the same evening and then take her there. Two days later the same ten or twelve friends of Johan Corneliussen's were again in action. Now they were moving house. First they picked up some belongings at the Sogn student village, then at Eva Linde's digs on Carl Berner's Place (Eva was nowhere to be seen), and drove them to Grorud. They carried the things up, and later there arrived delivery trucks from all kinds of obscure 'firms', bringing sofas, refrigerator, stove, TV, chairs, tables, curtains, bracket lamps, etc., etc. And they helped carry all of it up and put it in the right places – books in the bookcases, clothes in the wardrobes – they even helped hang the curtains. By evening the apartment was shipshape and ready to be occupied. Then they left, because Eva Linde would be coming at any moment. One week later there was a house-warming party. Then they finally saw Eva Linde. She stood in the hall welcoming the guests, and Elias Rukla (along with his compeers) thought she was as ethereally beautiful as the first time he saw her.

Johan Corneliussen and Eva Linde had moved in together. Into a three-room apartment located in a high-rise building at Grorud. This was the autumn of 1969. They were married around the New Year in 1970, and later the same year their baby daughter, Camilla, was born. In 1972, Johan Corneliussen took his PhD in philosophy, with a dissertation on the relationship between Marx and Kant. For various reasons it did not lead to his obtaining a position, so their economy must be said to have been poor. In 1976, therefore, Johan Corneliussen had apparently had enough, and he left his three-room apartment at Grorud, his still equally beautiful wife, and their six-year-old daughter, Camilla, never to return. Elias Rukla, who during this whole period had been a welcome guest in their home, in his capacity as Johan Corneliussen's close friend, was given the news by telephone from the Fornebu Airport. Johan told him that he had run away from it all, that he was now standing with an airline ticket to New York in his hand and would land in America within eight hours, in order to seek out a completely different future, and that this time it was not a matter of philosophy.

This did not come as a surprise to Elias at the time, although it was shocking news. Things had come to a standstill for Johan Corneliussen, not the least sign of which was his parting remark to Elias. Dumbfounded, Elias had gathered his wits about him to make a last-ditch appeal to his reason and said, But Eva . . . and Camilla? Then Johan Corneliussen had said, brusquely, I'm leaving them in your care, and hung up. Elias had been terribly put out, while clearly realising that this remark was part of a pattern. What had gone wrong for Johan?

In 1970, at any rate, there was a close happy family at Grorud. Eva and Johan and the newborn Camilla. In 1972, when Johan took his PhD in philosophy, he was lionised at the Institute of Philosophy, as was to be expected. But then nothing happened. Johan Corneliussen could not get anywhere. There was no vacancy at the Institute. He could have received a large and coveted fellowship at a German university and was urged to apply for it, but he never did. The practical problems were so difficult to deal with, he said, because if Eva and Camilla were to come along, the fellowship was too small, and if he were to go by himself and stay away for a year, maybe two years, no, it wouldn't work. And so he ended up sticking around, at home, as a half-time research fellow who, in addition, taught a course preparing students for their preliminary examination in philosophy. This gave him, when all the hours were added up, including university courses taught in other towns, away from home, in Kongsberg and Notodden, in Skien, Tønsberg and Fredrikstad, an acceptable annual salary, but no more. As far as Eva's education was concerned, it was a hit -and-miss affair. Her studies did not amount to much, and the end result was that she took a job as a secretary, full-time as long as Johan was at his busiest working on his PhD dissertation, later generally part-time. It was rather cramped behind the generous and glittering façade, cramped, always cramped, even in 1970, when happiness raised the roof, in a manner of speaking.

All that time, Elias was close to them, as the family friend, and especially Johan's friend. Every once in a while Johan would call and invite him to Grorud. And Elias Rukla went. Took first the tram from Majorstua to the National Theatre, underground , walked down Karl Johans gate from the National Theatre to Railway Square, where he took the T-bane to Grorud, entered the high-rise building and took the lift up to the ninth floor, where they were expecting him. It seemed to him he was part of everything they ever did. Dined with them, went on rambles with them, took part in the care of the baby (only as an interested spectator, to be sure), and he also went along, with both or with one of them, to the supermarket, where he insisted on sharing the bill, in return sticking his nose into what was to be purchased. It also happened that he stayed the night, on the living-room sofa. In the wintertime they went skiing in Lillomarka. Eva, Johan (with little Camilla in a reindeer sleigh), and Elias Rukla. Eva attracted enormous attention – the male skiers stopped instantly when she passed by, staring open-mouthed after her. They tried, all three of them, to ignore it, but at times Johan could not refrain from laughing, and so they would all three of them laugh, a bit resignedly, though Elias was unable to imbue his laughter with any authentic resignation, because, after all, he was also dazzled by Eva Linde's unearthly beauty. He would walk beside her, behind

Johan, who was pulling the reindeer sleigh. She saw to it that little Camilla did not have the sun in her face. Elias Rukla saw to it as well, all the while engaging in small talk. He liked the way she talked. Her voice, when she talked, had a certain timbre that came from way inside her vocal cords somewhere, something veiled, something he could not find words for and had never heard before. The attractive young woman searched for words, tasted them, as if asking herself, and not least others, and in this case Elias Rukla, who was walking beside her, behind Johan (who was pulling the reindeer sleigh with the small child), Can I really say this? Now and then she would laugh at something he said, quite exuberantly, which pleased Elias. But he could not say that he 'knew' her. No, that he could not say, he knew little or nothing about her, but even so he felt close to her, as a friend, not least in situations like this, where other men stared open-mouthed after her when the three of them, Johan (with Camilla on the sleigh), Eva and he, Elias Rukla, passed them by while skiing in Lillomarka. He experienced her as a beauty that had to be protected, also by him, Johan's friend. He was thrilled by the way she showed off her face. Which required the greatest thoughtfulness on his part not to say anything wrong, such as describing it in so many words, because he suspected she would not feel flattered but, quite the contrary, be irritated, and so strongly that she would dislike him, maybe even so strongly that she would speak ill of him to Johan Corneliussen. Accordingly, he was very discreet with her, in order not to offend what he assumed to be her fragile beauty. So he was mostly engaging her in conversation, trying to amuse her rather than get to know her. When all was said and done, he associated her beauty with being asleep. In his innermost self he associated Eva Linde's beauty with sleep. When she showed off her face, as when they went skiing in Lillomarka, it was clear, to be sure, purged of its origin in sleep, but at the same time it had an impersonal aspect, something she obviously could not help and therefore did not like to be remarked upon, he assumed, and so it was right, well, chivalrous, of Johan to laugh resignedly at those lingering glances and also for him, Elias, to join in this resigned laughter as best he could. But her beauty's home was in the repose of sleep, that was clear to him. Maybe it was because he so often experienced her precisely as being asleep, behind the door to her and Johan's bedroom in their Grorud apartment. After all, his connection with Eva Linde and Johan Corneliussen was based on the fact that he was Johan Corneliussen's friend, and Johan Corneliussen's friend from his bachelor days, when so many of their joint activities consisted of going on the spree together, through thick and thin, one might say, and that their friendship still consisted in going on the spree together, though not to the same extent as before. But Johan often met Elias in town. And, too, after closing time he often invited Elias to come along to Grorud to continue the bender. Then Eva would be asleep behind a closed door facing the living room. While Johan and Elias engaged in discussion and talked together. About life in general (that is to say, philosophy, literature, art, politics, etc., etc., and often with reference to their own lives). As a rule Elias would then stay the night on the living-room sofa, take the tram back to the city early in the morning, and go directly to his first class at Fagerborg. Before he hurried off, Johan had got up, along with little Camilla. Eva was still asleep. Her beauty sleep, he presumed. So that every time he really saw her, say, on Sundays when they went skiing in Lillomarka, she was in Elias' perception of her enveloped in an aura of sleep. With her soft face, satisfied and soothed by sleep, she belonged to the restfulness of sleep; that was where she came from, though he had never seen her sleep, only known that she was lying behind that closed bedroom door facing the living room, a rectangle clearly separate from the wall, with a doorknob a little below the middle, to the left, which Johan Corneliussen pressed down to let himself in at least once every time they sat like that on the ninth floor of a high-rise building at Grorud till late in the night, closed the door gently behind him, and then, shortly afterwards, came out again, but without saying anything. Johan Corneliussen's indescribably attractive wife. Johan Corneliussen and Elias Rukla in the living room. Johan Corneliussen going up to the window to look out. The lights below. The four-lane highway, illuminated, and now at night without a single car. The philosopher Johan Corneliussen who taught Elias Rukla so many things. Johan Corneliussen who talked and Elias Rukla who came out with objections, dry comments, trying to display a healthy scepticism towards Johan Corneliussen's deep-probing thoughts and ideas. They tried to speak in low voices, but now and then they became too excited, and one of them had to intervene and hush the other. But once when Elias hushed Johan Corneliussen in this way, the latter said, It's not necessary. She isn't sleeping anyway. She pretends to be asleep, but she's listening. I've caught her repeating conversations we've had when supposedly she was fast asleep. This made a strong impression on Elias Rukla. And every time since when he was at Grorud with Johan late at night, drinking and discussing with him, he kept thinking of her lying behind that door, immersed in sleep, enveloped by the soft shell of sleep, but listening. And his heart filled with sadness, because this woman who, lying there in the ambience and posture of sleep, was listening to the voices of her husband and the latter's friend, voices that, rising, sank into her slumbering consciousness, made Elias Rukla think about his own solitary situation. It must have been in 1974 that Johan Corneliussen suddenly came out with this statement about his young wife listening in her sleep, and Elias Rukla was then a bachelor of thirty-four and had long ago given up the idea of finding a life partner. Actually, he did not mind; he liked to be alone, and one of the reasons why he had always withdrawn from women (after he had asked them for a date and walked them home, at the moment when one usually tries to make an overture, Elias had done the opposite, held out his hand and thanked them for a lovely evening, often to the young lady's disappointment, he had noticed, though, to be sure, only after he got home) was, in fact, that he was afraid of losing himself by getting involved with someone who, all things considered, was a total stranger, with whom he would have to share everything, and the feeling of being smothered, held tight, which then rose in him, had been so strong that he had decided to live alone, as a bachelor, because that suited him best; but now and then he would be overcome by sadness, a feeling that he suffered from a lack, which not only made him contemptible in the eyes of others, for that he knew he was, but also made him a half-person, insofar as the drive towards 'the other' was absent from his life at the age of thirty-four. And so, here he sat on the ninth floor of a high-rise building at Grorud, in his friend's apartment, together with his friend, knowing he was half a person who would never be whole and feeling overcome with grief at the prospect of never becoming whole, inasmuch as he knew that behind that door lay Johan Corneliussen's wife, who made Johan Corneliussen whole, listening to her husband's (and the latter's friend's) voice in her slumbering state, and in this way, he thought, I steal into a woman's slumberous state, as the shadow of Johan Corneliussen that I am. And this he thought without bitterness, as an affirmation of the facts of the case, because these were, after all, the circumstances under which his life was lived, and by and large Elias Rukla thought at that time, in 1974, that he was living as rich a life as one might reasonably expect to live, with a meaningful job, great personal freedom, and an undiminished intellectual curiosity about life and the scope and limits that life defines for you, not least in a social perspective. And so, soon afterwards, he would take the sheet, duvet cover, and pillowcase that Johan Corneliussen handed him and begin to make a bed for himself on the sofa, preparing to stay the night as so often before, while Johan Corneliussen padded about the apartment, turned out the lights, and checked the electric switches before quietly disappearing into the bedroom, to his still-just-as-attractive wife, Eva Linde.

This was the situation. It was in 1974 that Johan Corneliussen had disclosed that Eva Linde used to listen to their conversations, giving them a different hue than before. Did Elias Rukla love Eva Linde? Did he lie on the sofa outside her and Johan Corneliussen's bedroom door for seven years waiting for her? No, Elias Rukla could honestly say that this was not so. It was simply unthinkable. He was taken with her, that he would admit, but it was as Johan Corneliussen's spouse that he was taken with her. She had no value at all for him by herself; that was not only forbidden, it was unthinkable. Had he then suffered from an unthinkable love for her? That was something Elias Rukla could not dismiss out of hand, and it would, if true, explain the twinges he used to feel in certain situations, of sadness, even grief, as well as a state of excitement, like the time when Johan Corneliussen disclosed that Eva Linde was listening to them behind her closed door. So it is not impossible that, between 1969 and 1976, from when he was twenty-eight until he turned thirty-six, when he started his career as senior master at the Fagerborg school in a mood of high expectation, established himself in an apartment of his own in Jacob

Aalls gate, tried, albeit somewhat half-heartedly, to find a life partner, not least among his younger colleagues at Fagerborg and other secondary schools, amused himself in his leisure time mixing with old acquaintances from his student days, cultivated and kept up his particularly close friendship with Johan Corneliussen – it is not impossible that, in reality, he was suffering from, and letting his steps be controlled by, an unthinkable love for Eva Linde. But if that was so, no trace of this love can be found anywhere, except possibly for those brief occasional twinges in the course of those seven long years, not even in the rather odd geographical fact that, when Elias Rukla and Johan Corneliussen met in town, they did not follow it up with an evening in Jacob Aalls gate but in remote Grorud, a suburban village a good six miles from downtown Oslo with its restaurants, forcing Elias Rukla to get up at the crack of dawn the next morning and leave in a hurry to get to his job as senior master, whereas if they had ended up in Jacob Aalls gate, Johan Corneliussen could have taken it easy, because he did not have such obligations early the next morning. But it was Johan who insisted that they should go to his place, and that was due to the fact that it was his job to take care of Camilla when she awoke in the morning (so that Eva could sleep), and so he had to get home. Therefore, if they were to continue, it had to be at his place. So it was not the sleeping Eva who tempted Elias Rukla to undertake this rather strange trip to Grorud, but the company of Johan Corneliussen. Nevertheless, Elias Rukla could not dismiss the possibility that he had all along suffered from an unthinkable love of Eva Linde, but, if so, it had not even once been allowed to control his anything but remarkable steps, and if something had not happened that was beyond his control, creating an entirely new situation, he could have lived his whole life, to this day, when this is being written, that is NOW, without his having had the least suspicion that he was suffering from an unthinkable passion, whose source was the gradually rather fading beauty Eva Linde Corneliussen.

It was in 1974 that Elias Rukla had felt this twinge of pain that made him wrought up, and subsequently wistful, at the thought that, behind the door where Eva Linde was asleep, there was a listening woman in a state of slumber. By that time, however, Johan Corneliussen must unconsciously have reached the decision that made Elias Rukla's unthinkable love thinkable. The proof of this is contained in his strange decision not to apply for the large fellowship that would have taken him and his family to the University of Heidelberg for two years. His justification was that the family could not afford it and that he did not want to go there by himself. Due to family reasons, that is, he decided not to apply for the fellowship (which he had been urged to apply for), something Elias, and many others, already then thought was odd, because the small family would have managed without any special problems, given the economic circumstances in which Dr Corneliussen, PhD, would find himself in Heidelberg. But this oddity also pointed to something else, something of much greater scope and seriousness: by this, Johan Corneliussen declared that he was no longer going all out for philosophy. Through this decision Johan Corneliussen showed (to those who wanted to see, which nobody did at the time) that he would no longer devote his life to becoming a contributor to nothing less than the dossier of human thought, which, after all, he had asserted that the literature about Immanuel Kant actually was. So something must have happened to Johan Corneliussen that was rooted in his thinking.

He took his PhD in philosophy in 1972, at the age of thirty. His dissertation on the relationship between Kant and Marx had been speeded up after he became a family man. He was very pleased to have finished, and he had asked Elias to read the dissertation before it was submitted for evaluation. Elias was honoured and read it, despite the fact that he was completely unqualified to do so. But he was stunned by the power of Johan Corneliussen's thinking. At the same time he had a sneaking little doubt, which he hesitated to express. Had Johan's transition from Kant to Marx taken place as smoothly as Johan had indicated in conversation with him (and others)? For even if Elias Rukla was completely unqualified to appraise this dissertation, he had wondered whether its very foundation was not rather vague. It belonged, of course, to the field that Johan Corneliussen, following his ambition, aimed to enter, namely, the literature on Kant, but all the same it appeared to be somewhat wavering with regard to whether it was written by a Kantian or a Marxist. Was it the literature about Kant (that is, Marx's relationship to Kant) or Marxism as an ideology of liberation that was Johan Corneliussen's principal concern in this dissertation? Elias Rukla could not tell for sure and felt rather perplexed, but, as already indicated, he hesitated to voice his doubt, both because he was not qualified to entertain such a doubt and also because he was afraid of offending his friend, for even if the doubt concerning his dissertation was expressed by an unqualified person, it might seem wounding to Johan Corneliussen, considering the situation in which he then found himself, he had assumed. However, Johan Corneliussen himself had no doubt about his being a Marxist; he was no longer a student leader, to be sure, or a political activist in any other way, yet in his fundamental thinking he was a Marxist, that he maintained. Anyway, his PhD dissertation was very well received in the Institute of Philosophy at Blindern, and Dr Corneliussen's future appeared very bright. Two years later he was urged to apply for the large fellowship that was to have taken him to Heidelberg, but then he said no. Why?

Did he have a doubt resembling the one which the unqualified reader, Elias Rukla, had had when he read his dissertation? Or did he decide not to apply for the fellowship because he feared he would not get it anyway? Was there in the appeal, which came from the highest authority at the Institute of Philosophy, an undertone of reserve that Johan Corneliussen had picked up? And had there not also been an undertone in the enthusiasm that his dissertation had aroused? Elias Rukla had been present at the candidate's mandatory academic lecture and participated in the subsequent celebration, and it had occurred to him, though just barely, just barely, by all means, that the homage offered to Johan Corneliussen was somewhat strained. Everyone seemed concerned to live up to the idea that this was a long-awaited event, but the ones who showed authentic enthusiasm, and therefore represented an absolutely necessary stimulus in the celebration of Johan Corneliussen's PhD degree, were those of his fellow students who considered his work to be a Marxist pamphlet. Johan Corneliussen had been captured by Marxism. Elias Rukla could not look at it in any other way when he recalled this celebration. Could it be that he was incapable of relating to Marxism with the same intellectual fervour he had felt previously, when he dreamed of entering the ranks of the inter-preters of Kant? That he was a Marxist there could be no doubt, but did Marxism manage to give him the same satisfaction, the same enduring joy of butting against the outer limits of thought he had felt when his mind was grappling with far-flung plans of taking his place among the long row of important philosophers who saw them-selves exclusively as interpreters of Kant? Elias Rukla wondered about that, and he wondered even more whether Johan Corneliussen did not wonder about it as well – in other words, whether this thought had not occurred to him and, of course, been dismissed, yet remained with him as a muted disappointment in his innermost self. To go back to the thinking of his early days as a student was impossible, as he considered the basis of Marx's historical materialism to be all too self-evident, and so he had been captured by Marxism even in his thinking, leaving him short of contemplative satis-faction, Elias Rukla thought. And, sure enough, when Johan Corneliussen used Marxism, say, in his nocturnal discussions with Elias Rukla on the ninth floor of the cramped three-room apartment in the high-rise building at Grorud, it had turned out to be primarily Marxism as a method of understanding *capitalism*. As time went on, Johan Corneliussen spoke little about Marxism as a vehicle of liberation. Thus, he more and more avoided terms like 'working class', for example, to the relief of Elias Rukla, incidentally. Though he had benefited, too; indeed, there is no denying that, personally, Elias Rukla greatly benefited from his discussions with Johan Corneliussen, because he could later draw upon them in his classes at Fagerborg Secondary School, both in his Norwegian and his history classes, sitting behind his desk in a classroom which at certain times was defined by pupils with a penchant for the same language as that of Dr Corneliussen, Doctor of Philosophy. No, what fascinated him was the superiority of Marxism for an understanding of the dominant social system in our part of the world. And then he was not just thinking of external factors, like class relations, power structures, etc., but first and foremost of Marxism as a vehicle for understanding the innermost dreams, hopes, disappointments, and secret desires of human beings deeply marked by capitalism. He was very much preoccupied with advertising, both as language and image. He had been so as long as Elias had known him, and with this as a starting point his transition to Marxism blended nicely with a greater depth in his understanding of the world in which it manifested itself. Already in the mid-1960s, Elias had wondered about Johan Corneliussen's relationship to advertising, such as when they found themselves in the highbrow Oslo cinema Gimle. There the usual thing was that the commercials before the film were greeted with laughter. Elias, too, used to laugh, but sitting there in the dark beside him Jonas Corneliussen was sucking up the advertising images, all alone, surrounded by bursts of laughter. It was as though he felt they were an expression of the art of our time. And of course they were, he afterwards asserted. The advertising images say more about our time than the art you find in the galleries, he maintained. Later, as a rebellious Marxist, he amplified his view. The art of the galleries was adapted to the taste of the wealthy public of the metropolises. Advertising, or commercial art, as he called it, pandered, with every possible means, to the taste of the large masses of people in the same metropolises. The fascination. He said it was a matter of understanding the very fascination which pulls us towards the darkness that capitalism is, intellectually understood, while it is perceived as glamour, glitter and gewgaws, which capitalism also is, if only you open your eyes and *see*. Shining, glittering, sparkling – look at any metropolis. After attending a big international philosophy conference in Mexico City, or Ciudad de Méjico, as he used to say, in early December 1975, he was even more taken up with this. Then he had seen for himself how the poor masses were streaming into the big city, bewitched by the idea of living just there. They left a poor, humdrum everyday life in the countryside for a hopeless slum on the fringes of the metropolis from which they would never escape. They had been better off where they came from, but they set out for the metropolis and dug in there. Why? The fascination. The fascination of being *contemporary* with the big cars, the TV programmes, the fancy restaurants, the lines of cars, the lights of the cinema ads, the lotteries, the luxurious residences behind high walls with armed guards outside the gate. Hunger might gnaw at their vitals, but being contemporary with the TV shows makes you forget it. The dreams quench the thirst. Dreams give satisfaction! he would exclaim in his cramped three-room apartment at Grorud in the middle of the night, and so loud that Elias said hush, hush, as they were used to do when one of them made the mistake of getting too deeply affected by his own words.

With this in mind, Elias Rukla was not surprised when, five months after Johan Corneliussen returned from the international philosophy conference in Mexico, he received his telephone call from Fornebu Airport just outside Oslo and was told that he was on his way to New York – for good. Johan told him that he was entering the service of capitalism (a sarcasm, or perhaps it is called irony). He was not greatly surprised. For Elias did not doubt that Johan Corneliussen was still a Marxist, and what was he to do with that fact? He did, after all, possess a unique understanding, namely Marxism, which gave him a superior ability to interpret people's dreams, once they found themselves where they did find themselves, here, in this society, that is. He could take advantage of this ability of his only by entering the service of capitalism, because capitalism is, after all, the only system that can turn these dreams to account and, not least, make use of dream interpreters. Marxism as such contains a moral element of an educational nature which is at variance with actually making use of this ability. But here was Johan Corneliussen telling him that he had been offered a dream job in New York. In a big consulting firm which had as its speciality to evaluate commercial ideas, concepts and designs, and whose clients were the big film companies, advertising agencies, book publishers and record producers. He would get rich, he said, in a strangely naive manner, and the moment he said it Elias Rukla wished wholeheartedly that Johan Corneliussen would get rich, although he also felt strangely disappointed, even cheated, that Johan would be gone for good and had not uttered a word about it beforehand. Only when he asked about Eva (and Camilla) and understood that they did not belong in Johan's new future, as a philosophical consultant and dream interpreter in the USA, did he feel shocked, not least because Johan said, I'm leaving them in your care, which he just then interpreted as a sarcasm, hurtful and bewildering.

It was planned. The pattern was clear. In any case, since 1974 Johan must subconsciously have entertained plans to abandon philosophy, and at the international philosophy conference in Mexico he must have established contacts that made this possible. He had known for five months that he was going to leave them, for good. And not said a word to Elias. Had he told Eva, and when? How long had they both known, and what had she done when she was told? He never found out, for when a little later he rang the doorbell at the apartment on the ninth floor of the high-rise building at Grorud, he found a woman who would never again mention Johan Corneliussen's name, or speak about him. But why did he leave her? That Elias never got to know, for not even at the time when they lived together did they let him in on the disagreements they must have had. The only thing he could ascertain was that Johan Corneliussen had left Eva, and not only Eva but also a daughter of six whom he obviously cherished above everything on earth, and since he did so, it must have been because his love had died. His love had died, and even though he cherished the child they had together more than anything in the world, it did not suffice to make him decide to take the child with him to the USA, because then he would also have to take along the child's mother, and his love was dead. How long had his love been dead? Johan Corneliussen's love, which had died. How long ago? It must have been dead when he returned from Mexico City and had made the decisive contact that made this leap possible. He had been planning it for five months, with his dead love behind the closed bedroom door, in the night, alone, or together with Elias Rukla (without saying anything), or other friends (also without saying anything, only thinking, racking his brains). Why, why? His love had died. But how was it possible that his love of Eva Linde could be dead?

And why this sarcasm directed at him, as the last word from friend to friend, before he quite simply put down the receiver? It made Elias feel confused, and it would continue to confuse him for years to come. For as it turned out, he was to occupy himself with Johan Corneliussen's sudden and final departure even though he had no-one he could talk to about it. Why this sarcasm, followed only by his putting down the receiver? Why end a friendship of many years with such an unkind break? Now and then it occurred to him that it was not at all meant as a sarcasm, but that it was the expression of a naive, slightly confused wish, and that Johan, after having expressed his wish, felt embarrassed and put down the receiver in sheer perplexity. Or that he put down the receiver because the plane he was taking, to London (with a change of planes to New York), was just being announced for the last time and he had to run to catch it. Yes, this is how Elias would think now and then in the years to come, but regardless of how much he thought, Johan Corneliussen's parting words left him at his wits' end. Time and time again he would also carefully go over, in his mind, the last five months Johan spent in Norway and the conversations he had had with Elias then, either alone on those evenings at Grorud, or in town, or whenever all three of them, Eva, Johan and he, had been together, but without being able to find the least hint of a sign Johan might have given him that he was about to leave them. He did find some possible signs, of course, and he brooded over them, but all such possible signs dissolved into nothing as soon as he began to analyse them specifically as signs from Johan to him, and so he had to conclude: Johan left no signs, no message, except perhaps for this sarcasm at the very end, just before he had to put down the receiver and make a dash for the plane. Elias Rukla was bewildered. He was at the Fagerborg school when Johan Corneliussen rang him up.

He took the telephone standing in the staff room. When Johan put down the receiver he understood nothing. He immediately went to the principal and asked to be released from his last three classes for the day, because something had happened to some intimate friends which required his presence, as he put it. Then he took the underground straight to Grorud.

Eva was home, and alone. She was calm, but a bit tired. She confirmed what had happened. It had all been settled. The separation papers signed by them both and all dispatched. There was no more to be said. As far as she was concerned, it would serve no purpose to talk any more about this. All the same she invited him for coffee, since he had come this long way to Grorud. Elias was astonished, even outraged, and showed it, first and foremost because he had not suspected anything. That . . . no . . . he understood nothing . . . and he was so bewildered that she started laughing. They were sitting side by side on the sofa, that was how she had set the table. Feeling concerned, Elias asked how she would manage, to which she replied that there would be no problems. As soon as she could see it all in perspective, that is. Well, yes, she was a bit tired, obviously. And suddenly she leaned her head against his shoulder. Yes, she put her head on his shoulder, making a strange shudder go through Elias Rukla, utterly different from anything he had previously experienced. No, no, he thought, this cannot be true, and to reassure himself about that, and to escape from this strange feeling that flowed through him, he discreetly patted her hand in all friendliness. They sat like that for a while, she with her head on his shoulder, he filled with a rapture he could not believe in, until he got up and said he had to go.

Bewildered and jittery, and driven by this unaccustomed rapture he had admittedly felt filling him to the brim, three days later he rang her up and invited her for dinner. They met in Petit, at Majorstua, and from the way she looked at him, addressed him, came forward and smiled at him, he understood that what before had been unthinkable had now become thinkable, and she walked back with him to his apartment in Jacob Aalls gate and stayed the night. Elias Rukla was then thirty-six years of age and could only shake his head at all the happiness which had so suddenly befallen him.

Now many things happened in a short time. Eva moved with her little daughter into Elias Rukla's apartment in Jacob Aalls gate, which was not the small three-room apartment, but a larger four-room place he had acquired by exchange in the same neighbourhood, well, street. That had happened even before Johan Corneliussen had set himself up in his new life in New York. A couple of years later they were married, but Eva kept her name, Linde, her maiden name so-called. Master Rukla must be described as a man contented with his lot as he made his way, light of foot, in thin shoes, to his daily task at the Fagerborg school, up Jacob Aalls gate, past the mud puddles of the mild spring thaw in the month of March, around 1978, and later as well, in spite of the fact that Eva Linde never, not with a single word, said that she loved him. He could not understand why she didn't, but since she moved in with him, into the new apartment he had acquired, and afterwards agreed to marry him, she must have loved him, but for some reason or other could not say she did. Was it because she feared that he would not believe her if she said it? Was it because it would elicit more questions on his part, about things which had happened that she would refuse to talk about, because it was over, finished? He did not know. But she had come to him, and it was she who had taken the initiative to become intimate. In the morning he ate breakfast with his wife, who was radiantly beautiful, and her rather capricious daughter. That was his new life. In the afternoons and evenings they were together, mostly in the apartment, while her daughter was running back and forth. He slept with her at night, in a private room in the apartment on Jacob Aalls gate furnished for that purpose – yes, this is how he would express it, because to say that he slept with her in the bedroom, or in their shared bedroom, covered so little of what he felt about sleeping with Eva Linde that, to himself, he always called their bedroom 'that private room which has been furnished for my sleeping with her', and if it sounded pompous, he would still describe it that way to himself, because this was the way it had to be described, although not in front of others, including Eva, whom it might make embarrassed, just as embarrassed as he would find her to be during intercourse now and then, when she gave herself to him but often with her face half turned away, and he could not tell for certain whether it was an expression of her nature or of something completely different, causing him at times to gasp out, I love you I love you. Then she might stroke the back of his head, or his shoulders, while she *looked* at him, straight into his eyes though without saying anything, but the fact that she stroked him was sufficient then. At that moment she belonged to him. By the way, she would spend much time in this room, the so-called bedroom, as she had her make-up table there. Both there and in the bathroom were little flasks, tubes, bottles, lipstick, boxes, all lined up, and in such numbers as to make Elias Rukla inclined not to believe his own eyes. She had come to him. Gradually he became acquainted with her. She came to him with several albums of photographs. She sat down on the sofa and showed them to him. Photographs from her youth, which she (eagerly) showed him while telling him about them. Snapshots. From Hønefoss. From the lower Setesdal valley. From a village north of Lillehammer. Bardu. An officer's daughter growing up in Norway in the 1950s. For him, these photo albums became a treasure chest. They became so very dear to him. He felt honoured to have been chosen to sit like this, looking at photographs from her youth while she eagerly related, with the fervour of recognition in her voice, and he could not help but regard living in the state of marriage as a mystery, on the basis of sitting beside her on the sofa looking at snapshots like this and hearing her repeat the rather banal story behind each of them in a veiled voice. The way to her. The completion of their sexual life, which spread out, taking on the form of a shared everyday life. The daily absorption in, the daily occupation with. Rather than being able to say that he knew her, Elias Rukla could say that he found himself in circumstances where he was occupied with her every day, even when he did not see her, and that he assumed, almost as a matter of course, that it was mutual. She had come into his life, and that shaped his consciousness in a deeply satisfying way. There were many things he did not know about her, which she kept to herself, but what he did get to know was a source of enduring happiness to him. He might see a certain kind of chocolate at the tobacconist's stand and think, Eva likes that one, and another chocolate and think, That one Eva turns up her nose at. He knew that she preferred tea in the evening, and strong, all too strong, coffee in the morning. He knew what she liked to eat and when, and what she did not like to eat. He knew in what way she was unsure of herself, and how she was able to hide it. Simple, commonplace tricks, which he appreciated finding out about, because it attached her to him, with her unreserved consent. And he was confident that she had come to know him the same way. That all the trifles which he himself, on the whole, did not care very much about, such as his preferring potato chips with paprika, not onions, to go with beefsteak, that he disliked showering in the morning and therefore did it in the evening instead etc., etc., that all these things, in themselves insignificant trifles which he could easily have dispensed with if it had not been for the fact that they had simply turned into habits, unshakeable habits, which he nevertheless did not define as a necessary part of his own identity, were, for her, inseparably connected with being Elias Rukla. And she related intimately to them, so that she made him happy buying potato chips with paprika and serving beefsteak without onions, just as he accepted and was delighted with her habits, giving her what he knew she liked; and although she also, on the whole, regarded these things as rather insignificant, nevertheless this was what united them, this was their interlinked life, in joy, this was the way they lived together and thought about one another. Having turned thirty-six before a woman entered his life in earnest, Elias Rukla set immense store by precisely this, not hesitating to designate it as the mystery of matrimony. He enjoyed the opportunity of pondering what to tell her when he came home, which episodes he should tell her about, and he looked forward to seeing her expression when he would tell her just this, because, he thought, This I certainly believe Eva will be glad to hear! Thousands of hours were spent on such considerations, and thousands of hours were spent on automatic explanations, deliberations, reflections, which he wasn't even aware he was making, but which were as a whole directed at her and determined his steps, totally. In the middle of a conversation, say, with a colleague in the staff room, or in the middle of a class, he would suddenly catch himself thinking, I have to remember to remind Eva that tonight there is a film with Jack Nicholson which will be discussed in the Film Magazine on TV (he had seen a notice in *Dagbladet* about it), even though there was nothing in the situation, either as regards his colleagues in the staff room or in his teaching, that could reasonably produce associations in this direction; they were just happy thoughts that popped up, as if to bless his life as a married man. Yes, he had got to know her. And she had let him do so unreservedly, also in roles that were not directly connected with their relationship. She let him freely enter her life as mother (of Camilla), as daughter (with her parents), and as friend (with her women friends, who often visited them), and in the role of his own wife when she stood properly by his side as he proudly introduced her to his colleagues. She had come to him, and she stayed with him. Why, he did not know, but she had come to him and stayed with him. She never said she loved him, but when he had asked her whether she would move in with him if he bought the larger apartment in Jacob Aalls gate, she said yes and came, and when two years later he proposed that they should get married, she looked at him, thought it over carefully, gave him a smile and said yes. But she added that she was Eva Linde. And just then Elias Rukla had thought, Yes, she's Eva Linde, and I will never get to know why she wants to live with me. But her wanting to is enough, actually more than enough; I'm delighted that she wants to, in spite of the fact that I will never know the reason why she wants to, and it is not certain that the reasons are the same as I wish they would be.

She tried to show him that she appreciated him. Often in a touching way. For example, by spoiling him in the matter of taking care of his clothes. Though she was absolutely not the domestic type, she insisted on ironing his shirts, pressing his trousers, and brushing his jackets. While he sat at his writing table correcting papers, she would stand at the ironing board in the living room, ironing and pressing, very fecklessly, quite helplessly, in fact, humming and singing like a genuine housewife (in reality, she was a part-time secretary and, on the side, still a student). When she was finished, she displayed the pressed trousers with a delighted smile. Or the freshly ironed shirts before she folded them. She brushed his suits – every time he was going to put on a suit, she brushed it beforehand. Indeed, she took care of his clothes as if it were a matter of priceless treasures; he had never asked her to, and she had not needed to do it, but she had taken it on, from the very first day, as a problem that she solved and was very pleased to solve. Could it be that she really would have preferred to be in an entirely different place, but that there she could not possibly be, and since she could not be where she most of all would have liked to be, she preferred to be where she was now, with him, and was that the reason for her silence? Oh, if that was the case, oh, Eva Linde, then, please, stay here. And Elias Rukla got up from his writing table and his pile of papers, walked over to her as she stood by the ironing board and gave her a big hug. Thanks for pressing my trousers. Thanks for ironing my shirts. Thanks for everything you have given me. As time went by, Elias Rukla used extreme caution in regard to expressing his love, for it had turned out that, when he did, she was not able to answer back with the same words, and then Elias knew he ought to refrain from doing so, and although it was very hard for him to hold back, he felt it was the right thing to do. And so, that was how they communicated:

she by smiling at him, his newly pressed trousers in her hands, he by getting up from his writing table, going over to her and giving her a big hug.

That was how they lived. Elias Rukla took great care in dealing with her, in order not to put her in an awkward position. Now and then, when she thought she was unobserved or forgot that he was present, she would gaze absently into vacancy, and in those moments she had a mournful expression on her face, looking unhappy, indeed. But as soon as she became aware that she had fallen into a reverie, and that he was in the room, she changed her expression to the direct opposite, smiling at him and trying to erase the expression she had inadvertently made the mistake of showing him, with the result that Elias was in despair, for he could not understand why she had to hide from him that she had felt unhappy for a moment; even if, deep down, she felt unhappy all the time, she did not have to hide it from him, because he could accept it as the way things were, together with his own powerlessness to help her with it. But in the morning she was not capable of dissembling. Eva Linde never wished to see another day; she did not want to wake up, holding so stubbornly on to her sleep that it appeared odd. It is her nature, Elias Rukla thought, she must have been that way all along, she has always preferred sleep to being awake, that's why she appears so fragile to her surroundings.

Actually she was a bit pampered. She had a spoiled air about her, which was inseparably linked to her indescribable beauty and regarded by herself with contempt, and yet she was unable to liberate herself from it, because being spoiled was agreeable to her, insofar as it elicited the desire to wait on her on the part of the person who was nearby when this trait flared up, blazing within her. She was pampered, and it showed continually. But only in brief glimpses. They were not well off. Elias Rukla was a senior master with student and housing loans to pay off, and a senior master's salary has never been high, and in Norway at that time, towards the end of the 1970s, it was relatively lower than ever. He had to pinch pennies, that was the bitter truth. Eva had to continue to work as a secretary at the Oslo Cinemas, part-time, and the studies she had given up a long time ago were never picked up again, in spite of the fact that this was what she really wanted to do. But she continued to work as a secretary without a murmur, doing so gladly, in fact, since it was her necessary contribution to their joint economy. However, suddenly she would snarl at him. Once it happened when Eva had set her heart on getting a new kitchen and had come home with a number of brochures. Then Elias had said it was out of the question. They simply could not afford it (they had bought a car half a year earlier). Then she snarled, Damn skinflint! at him, sending him a look filled with contempt. Yes, contempt. Undisguised contempt. For two or three seconds Elias Rukla looked into the eyes of an indescribably beautiful woman who harboured a boundless contempt for him, until she abruptly turned, completely around, and said in a gentle voice, I'm sorry, I know we can't afford it, it was silly of me. And the rest of the evening she was friendliness incarnate, and when they were going to bed she gave him clear signals that, if he wanted to come to her, there was nothing that would please her more, and if he came he could be certain of being well received.

This troubled Elias Rukla. Not that she looked hatefully at him, but her complaisance afterwards. Why did she not acknowledge her contempt for him, a man who was not equal to providing her with a new kitchen, now that the old one was so worn and old-fashioned? She was entitled to demand it of him, and although he had to tell her they could not afford it, he perfectly understood, even so, that she was entitled to despise him for it. If you marry a woman like Eva Linde, it brings certain obligations, which he had failed to fulfil by having to say no to her extremely commonplace dreams. He could say, of course, that she should have known what she was doing when she married an ordinary senior master with a limited income, and so he was safe when he said that a new kitchen at this point was out of the question, but at the same time he ought to have warned her, telling her that a woman like her could never have her wishes and dreams fulfilled by a rather threadbare secondary school teacher, something that, if he had told her, would have made her burst into unrestrained silvery laughter. She knew what she was doing. But had she for that reason written off her own worth as the woman whom Elias Rukla valued so highly? Precisely by showing her contempt when he had to admit that he could not afford to satisfy an extremely ordinary wish of hers, she showed, indeed accentuated, her value, placing her at the level where Elias Rukla himself thought she should be. So Elias Rukla had no problem accepting her contempt. What he had a problem accepting was her attempt to conceal it by glossing over it afterwards. Her deliberate complaisance afterwards. What brought it on? Why did she not dare maintain her contempt? Because she had signed away all right to it? That was quite obvious, but what did it mean? That she had signed away the right to make demands on him altogether, in her heart? And what, in turn, did that mean? Elias did not know, but he felt profound despair at her false complaisance after such outbursts and, as a matter of fact, found it difficult to respond to her invitation and come to her at night, which was, after all, as she had unequivocally signalled to him, what would please her most of all, and which he, for that very reason, could not refuse but, on the contrary, had to force himself to prepare for, as the great and, on the whole, quite undeserved honour which in that way fell to his lot, and which made it possible to describe Elias Rukla in these years as, if not a contented or happy man, at all events a lucky one.

Little Camilla, Johan Corneliussen's daughter, had moved into the newly purchased four-room apartment in Jacob Aalls gate along with Eva Linde. She became Elias Rukla's stepdaughter. She lived there, together with them, from the age of six to nineteen. One can safely say that Elias Rukla had never got to know any other person as well as Camilla Corneliussen. He followed her growing up near at hand, as an always-present stepfather. Elias and Eva Linde never had a child together, so Camilla was the only child he would ever watch growing up. About Camilla he could say that she did not need to worry about having secrets from him, at least as far as her nature was concerned, for he knew her inside out. He had seen her express herself freely and uninhibitedly as a child and adolescent and turn, with much hullabaloo, into the young lady she was today. Through her he experienced a child's fear of not being like everyone else, down to the minutest detail. He understood that this apprehension was even greater than the dread of being locked up in a dark room, which also was great and fundamental. And he came to understand the fear a little child can have that her shoe buckles, which she herself thinks are very pretty, do not look in the least like the buckles other children have on their shoes, that it can be a real torture to a little child's soul, and for a long time, and this gave him a good deal to think about. How will she be able to develop into an independent person under such conditions? he had often to ask himself during Camilla's adolescence. And it did not improve matters, quite the contrary, that the little child was at the same time extremely open and trusting with those around her, both with Elias and her mother, and even with those same children she was so afraid of not resembling to a T. What disasters, real and imagined, must this not lead to! And, sure enough, Elias witnessed all of little Camilla's disasters and breakdowns near at hand. When her mother's patience was exhausted, Elias stepped in, trying to soothe, encourage and comfort. And when Camilla entered her teens, he had to assume the role of mediator and reconciler between mother and daughter. He had a tendency to side with Camilla, for he thought that Eva Linde sometimes did not quite manage to distinguish between being Camilla's mother and educator and being her mother and owner. For that matter, it had started right after they got together. Camilla had then been given her own room, which she kept in all the years she lived with them, though its appearance changed quite radically as time went on, and Elias felt that neither of them had the right to go in there unannounced. He was of the opinion that a child was entitled to have its own room and to be left alone there, without fear of being disturbed by grown-ups. Eva did not agree with that, and over the years they had a number of arguments about this, but though Elias was inclined to give in to Eva on other matters concerning Camilla – after all, she was her daughter – he did not do so in this regard. But Camilla often sought his company. He had felt terribly sorry for the little girl when, at six years of age, she came padding after her mother, a teddy bear under her arm, in order to settle in his place. He had a feeling that she had been deprived of something in her life, and that the sense of loss left by what she had been deprived of, a father, was irremediable. And he did not himself want to remedy it, not even if he had been able to. He was Camilla's stepfather, taking the place of her father, but he could not replace that father, because he was not her father; her father was called Johan Corneliussen and lived in New York. Elias Rukla was her mother's friend and new husband, and in that capacity he was to take her father's place with Camilla. He did not for a moment wish to deprive Camilla of the sense of loss left by her father; that he had no right to do. Therefore he was always slightly reserved with her. When she came to him trustingly, wanting him to fulfil all her expectations, he had to take care to maintain a certain distance from her. In the same way, he found himself in a distant relationship with Eva's parents, the retired colonel and his wife. Their purpose in coming to see the married couple Rukla/Linde was, after all, to have contact with their grandchild, Camilla Corneliussen. In such circumstances Elias Rukla was an intruder, and accordingly kept in the background as far as possible when they visited the colonel and his wife or were visited by them, as, for example, at Christmas, and he had the impression that Eva's parents looked upon him as a man who, for the time being, was taking care of their daughter, even after they were quietly married, something that, per se, seemed natural to Elias Rukla. But in such circumstances, especially on Christmas Eves with the colonel's family in Lillehammer, which Elias Rukla did not exactly look forward to, he was always a bit apprehensive that Camilla would come over to him, as she often did at home, and sit on his lap, and when she did, he tried to coax her away as quickly as possible by some diversionary manoeuvre or other, not least because under the Christmas tree there lay a big package from Johan Corneliussen.

Because one year after they had begun living together, Johan Corneliussen had manifested himself. He wrote a letter to his daughter. Camilla had then just started school, and her mother took the letter to her room and read it to her there. Elias never learned what it said. He insisted, though, that Camilla answer it, which Eva did not want.

But Elias forced it through, and he sat for long periods with little Camilla composing a letter to her father, the way she herself would have written it if she had learned the art of writing letters. That she had not done, however; she could only write capital letters and had difficulty putting them together into words, which had a tendency to exceed the space of her sheet of paper when they were to make a whole sentence. So Elias had to help her, both with getting out of her the sentences she wished to write to her father and, later, with getting them down on paper in such a way that there was enough room for them. When this was done, at last, there remained the laborious task of preparing the envelope, on which Camilla would write her father's name and address. Eva, as indicated, refused to have anything to do with this letter-writing, and Elias could not bring himself to write Johan Corneliussen's name and address on an envelope which contained a letter to him from his daughter. So the only solution was that Camilla had to do it. But it took time to put the rather extensive address of Johan Corneliussen, written in a child's handwriting, in place on the rather small surface that an envelope provides, and it can at least be said that Camilla learned to discipline her childish capital letters in a manner that was unusual among children her age. Afterwards, more letters arrived, and the same procedure was repeated, until Camilla had become big enough both to be able to read her father's letters and to answer them on her own. She would sit undisturbed in her room writing letters to a father she barely knew, but who would haunt her entire life like a loss that nothing could soothe, Elias

Rukla thought. When she was fourteen, she was invited to New York to visit her father and her half-siblings, born to Johan Corneliussen in his third marriage. Eva Linde protested strongly against her daughter going, but again Elias managed to persuade her. But when they stood on the roof at the Gardermoen Airport and saw Camilla pad out to the large jumbo jet that was to carry her to New York, Elias Rukla felt fear take hold of him. What if she never came back, what if she writes to tell us that from now on she wants to stay with her father! He had already noticed that she now and then wrote her name as Camilla Cornelius, from her father's new name, which was John Cornelius, though not on anything official; but it said Camilla Cornelius on her pencil case, and she would scribble Camilla Cornelius on slips of paper strewn about everywhere, half in jest, but also to try out another identity, one that was more directly linked to her American father than Camilla Corneliussen, a name that Johan Corneliussen himself had dropped, and now Camilla, too, would drop Corneliussen and follow him as a Cornelius – at least she was trying it out, scrawling it down time and again, as he had noticed. Still, he insisted, and forced through, that she would go to New York that summer. He could not help it. With what right was he to prevent Johan Corneliussen from seeing his daughter again after eight years of being separated from her? With what right was he to prevent his stepdaughter from seeing her father again, after a whole lifetime, which after all it was to her? But fear took hold of him. Eva will not ever forgive me for this, he thought, and why should she? Johan

Corneliussen has done nothing to earn this, he thought, and it would be bloody unfair to Eva. He cannot do this to us, he thought. But all summer he was afraid that this was exactly what Johan Corneliussen could do. Elias Rukla knew Johan Corneliussen's exuberant personality, and what fourteen-year-old girl could resist this father when he displayed himself in his dazzling new surroundings? Poor Camilla, he thought, it is asking too much of you to be strong enough to resist. But Johan Corneliussen cannot do it, he thought. If he wants to, though, he will do it, leaving us behind, to sit here alone, for which I cannot ever be forgiven. What power that man has over us, he exclaimed, and for the first time he felt resentment against Johan Corneliussen and his entire person. But the summer went by. And Camilla came back again, to them, to stay with them in Jacob Aalls gate for the remainder of her growing-up years. At nineteen, after getting her final graduating exams, she left her childhood home to begin her professional education.

It was the year 1989. Elias Rukla was a quiet-mannered Norwegian secondary school teacher who had not distinguished himself in any way whatsoever in his life, which did not bother him, since he had never imagined he would distinguish himself in any way. He was an average, socially oriented Norwegian citizen who read his newspapers, watched TV, read his books and had his thoughts, and went to his job at Fagerborg Secondary School every day. The only sensational aspect of his life seemed to be that he had acquired such an attractive wife at thirty-six years of age, thirteen years ago. That was clear to him from the many surprised glances that brushed his face when he appeared with Eva Linde and could introduce her as his wife. Incidentally, her beauty was now greatly faded. She had spread out a good deal, and she had lost her charm. Elias Rukla did not much mind. True, his heart would sink when looking at photographs of Eva thirteen years ago and comparing them with the woman in her mid-forties he was married to, who shared the same identity but little else. A sensitive awareness of life's transitoriness, apropos of Eva's lost charm. Sadness. And the loss of the surprised glances, which he had to admit he missed, because everyone regrets having his own lustre wear off, and that was, of course, what happened when Eva lost her lustre, for then it was he, above all, who lost it, vis-à-vis the others. These are things that count, Elias Rukla thought, when he sat in the living room by himself in the evening, with his beer and his aquavit. He would sit thus quite often. As the years passed, his inclination to overindulge in drink had increased. Now he would sit up in the evenings after Eva had gone to bed. It had become a habit which had a calming effect on him; he needed a bit of time to himself, with his aquavit and his beer. For something had happened to him which he had difficulty understanding, as well as resigning himself to. It was a slowly growing sense of having been socially put out of the running. He was greatly troubled by it, and he thought it was quite extraordinary that it should be this way. But it was as though little of what was offered him as a socially conscious individual was still of sufficient interest to him. Neither TV nor the papers managed to stimulate him any longer. He had difficulty giving a rational answer to why they didn't. Anyway, they didn't. Time and again he told himself, It isn't that bad, after all. The newspapers have both news and culture pages, so what am I moaning about? And was it so much better before? No, it was not. People have always complained about the newspapers, and not least about TV, me too. But when, the next morning, he opened another paper, he had the same feeling of having been left out. What should have interested him, the day's news and the culture pages, was not able to engage him sufficiently, and he just leafed through the paper, often with an irritated gesture. The same with the TV. When he sat down to follow a TV debate, it was the same way. What the debaters said barely interested him, even if, to start with, Elias Rukla was interested in the topic that was to be debated, so interested every once in a while, in fact, that he was looking forward to the debate. The sole benefit he reaped came from studying the rhetorical skills of the partici- pants, their semantic tricks and carefully selected costumes, and then 'unmasking' them, but not even that afforded him the least pleasure, especially when he reflected that this was the only benefit he had derived. Hence, disappointment. The debaters did not address themselves to him at all, but to others who were obviously a far more important audience to be reached than him. But was that really something to moan about, namely, that he no longer received any pleasure from newspapers and TV? For Elias Rukla it was, because it influenced his daily mood, indeed, his fundamental mood as a socially conscious individual, and to an alarming degree. That what the papers played up as unique, sensational, important or noteworthy met with no sympathy from him but, on the contrary, the direct opposite, so that he either found it totally indifferent, totally alien, or even revoltingly stupid, made him, after being repeated day after day, month after month, year after year, quite simply feel very sad. And when supplemented by the fact that what he, Elias Rukla, was interested in was not to be found in the paper at all or – and this was almost worse – was hidden away in a brief notice, it made him feel like an outlived and decrepit human being. He felt as if he were no longer capable of keeping track of his own time, and no-one has ever felt like that without experiencing grief, perhaps also anger. He looked at pictures of individuals who were supposed to be famous and who had recently done something or other, but what they were famous for said nothing to him and did not impress him in the least, and the particular feat they had just performed appeared rather insignificant to him, while what meant something to him had to be searched for, like something hidden away, at best. It was the papers' hierarchical system that revolted him and made him feel regret. It was that those who set the tone in society judged and reflected reality in a manner that felt like a degradation of everything he stood for, shutting him out every day and forcing him to admit that, for him, the newspapers and TV signified a daily encounter with a never-ending personal defeat. Don't you ever get enough! he occasionally had to exclaim to himself. Can't you spare us! he entreated to himself, though knowing full well that it was a matter of free choice whether to read the paper and watch TV, but it was not that simple. For as a socially conscious individual he needed to engage with the world, understand it, be interested in it, participate with fervour and zeal in what society at large, through newspapers and TV, was occupied with, communicate, as it was called, except that it had become impossible for him to do so. I'll just give one example, he said to himself, as he paced the floor at night, up and down, in the living room of his home at Jacob Aalls gate, after Eva had gone to bed. In 1970 I attended a literary seminar in Finland, and then I became acquainted with the writings of Penti Saarikoski, which I later became deeply absorbed by. And I was not the only one who had a high opinion of him; he was generally acknowledged as one of Scandinavia's greatest contemporary authors. But when Penti Saarikoski died, only in his early forties, there appeared not a single word about him in the Norwegian papers. That Elias Rukla was aware of it at all was due to his overhearing a casual remark half a year later. But when a Swedish TV entertainer died not long afterwards, it was not only reported in the Norwegian dailies but given extensive front-page coverage. Not to mention the time when a Norwegian newscaster died. Then the papers declared a state of national mourning. Not even faced with death do they pause to reflect any longer. To collect their wits, show a bit of humility, pose a couple of the questions every human being *must* pose, unless you decide at the start to say to hell with the whole kit and caboodle, Elias Rukla said to himself, alone with his social suffering this evening, which now is turning into night. When a newscaster dies it is a private matter: her death is her family's grief, with which they should be left alone; it is of no public interest, for no newscaster, not even for TV, leaves behind anything of such great value, measured by the value of other human beings, that her demise transcends the parameters of the private sphere and turns into a national concern. But the newspapers did turn it into a national concern. It makes me vomit, Elias Rukla thought. How can this have happened? What has actually happened? Yes, what is going on? I do know what is going on, of course, Elias Rukla interjected to himself. Think of Hokksund. How many people at Hokksund care that Penti Saarikoski has died in his early forties? Twenty? But how many in Hokksund knew the TV newscaster, and even knew beforehand that she was ill? Four thousand? Five thousand? The answer is self-evident. But not the question. The fundamental question. And since the fundamental question is not posed, the unbearable answer is self-evident and inevitable. That's the way it is, he said out loud. Why can the fundamental question no longer be posed? Oh, I decline to answer that, he exclaimed, because everyone knows. Must I say it? No, I decline, he repeated obstinately. Instead he thought about his own life and work. If there was someone who had *proven* his loyalty to this society, it was he. For seven years he had devoted his life to study so as to prepare himself to be a public educator of Norwegian youth. Afterwards he had for nearly twenty-five years had as his daily task to convey the nation's self-understanding and fundamental values to the coming generation. He had done it all voluntarily, with open eyes; yes, it was his own decision, having chosen freely among many other possibilities that had been at his disposal, like becoming a lawyer, an engineer, economist, or doctor, etc., etc., but he had chosen to study philology in order to become one of the nation's loyal educators, carrying forward the foundation which all of society was built on, and had to be built on, in his view, a choice made without much pondering, to be sure, because it had been so self-evident. For twenty-five years he had faithfully endeavoured to fulfil his life's work as an ordinary and unassuming senior master, on a rather meagre salary. On the face of it a somewhat grey existence, as the monthly pay cheque clearly underscored. But that he had known beforehand, so he could not complain now that he had not become as well-to-do as a lawyer. His choice had been made on the premise that it would give him an inner satisfaction to have his day's work as a teacher in secondary school and that this satisfaction would produce an inner light which made the greyness of his outward appearance fairly unimportant, an assumption that showed a confidence in Norwegian society and its foundation that he had to characterise as touching, even beautiful, he thought, and which had been shared by surprisingly many young students in his own 1960s, as well as both before and after that decade – well, this touching confidence had, as a matter of fact, been general among talented young people throughout our nation's history, he thought, with some surprise, because he had never thought of it in that way before. Consequently, he felt deeply hurt that the papers and the TV no longer addressed themselves to him and those like him. It was as though the shapers of public opinion were not paying attention to him at all any more. On the contrary, they seemed to make a point of looking straight past him, almost as if it gave them a special pleasure to do so. He had become nothing to them, and Elias Rukla found that to be deeply wounding. Damn it all, he thought, I am, after all, an average, socially conscious individual, with a good education and a tolerably sound judgment. I am widely read, too. So why have I become so uninteresting to those who set the tone that they cannot even bring themselves to greet me any longer? Yes, that's how it felt to Elias Rukla. To put it quite simply, the newspapers wounded his vanity, because when he read them he understood how foolish it had been of him, with his possibilities, to become a secondary school teacher. It would never have happened today, he thought, as he had clearly told Camilla, his stepdaughter, last year. In any case, do not become a secondary school teacher, he had said, do not shut yourself up in a school. If you absolutely must, let it be solely because you cannot take the trouble to become anything else. I mean this in all seriousness, he had told his stepdaughter before she moved away from home. He felt defeated. Everything he stood for had been removed from everyday public discourse. Night after night, after Eva had gone to bed, he paced the floor of his apartment in Jacob Aalls gate, thinking about this. Had a few shots of aquavit, which he washed down with beer, taking great care not to have too much, for he did not want to show up at school with a hangover, though it happened now and then that he had too much all the same. Oh dear, he thought then, as he was about to turn in, realising it had been too much despite everything. He would get quite stirred up at times by such thoughts. The worst of it was that he felt he no longer had anything to say. Except to himself. An era had come to an end, and here he sat talking to himself. An era had come to an end, and Elias Rukla as a socially conscious individual along with it, because he had, after all, put himself at the disposal of that very era, as a public educator. He felt but little desire to be the educator of a new epoch, nor did he have the qualifications for it, to put it mildly. It's that simple, he exclaimed. That's the way it is, hell, yes. Decline on all sides. Just turn around, he exclaimed. Damn it all, you can't even talk any longer. When was the last time you had a conversation with someone? It must have been years ago, he decided after a moment's reflection. To find what means something to you, you have to grope your way through a mess of business interests, he added. You can be struck dumb by less. But they call this mess democracy. And if I call it a mess, they come and tell me that I have contempt for the people, he thought indignantly. And perhaps they are right, he reflected. Maybe I no longer believe in democracy. Oh, Elias, cut it out, will you? Now you're drunk, he said sternly to himself, and to be on the safe side he said it aloud, to hear whether he spoke with a slight snuffle, which he discovered to his relief that he did. But it was repeated. Time after time Elias Rukla caught himself late in the evening, after midnight, having such thoughts, and it made him feel depressed every time. That too! The fact that he was no longer even a democrat in his heart! What was the next thing going to be! Was it because he had been defeated? That the cause of his social suffering was the democratisation of culture and even of life itself? But he was against it, after all! He felt revolted by it! If so, if in fact the manifestations of democracy revolted him, why should he be a supporter of democracy? You are drunk, Elias, he again heard him saying to himself, go to bed, the night is wearing on. But he did not go to bed. He went on thinking, as deeply as possible. He tried to console himself with the thought of how common it was that a defeated, nearly annihilated minority found it difficult to acclaim those who defeated them, and the weapons that were used to vanquish them so utterly. But that duty was incumbent on him, insofar as it was the people's voice and people's right to express themselves which had defeated him. I refuse to consider myself undemocratic, he thought obstinately. That I will not put up with. And so, when the chips are down, I must say, though not without a sense of repugnance, that if you wish to show your belief in democracy, you also have to do so when you are in the minority, convinced both intellectually and, not least, in your innermost self, that the majority, in the name of democracy, is crushing everything that you stand for and that means something to you, indeed, all that gives you the strength to live and endure, well, that gives a kind of meaning to your life, something that transcends your own rather fortuitous lot, one might say. When the heralds of democracy roar, triumphantly bawling out their vulgar victories day after day so that it really makes you suffer, as in my own case, you still have to accept it; I will not let anything else be said about me, he thought. Then he went on sitting there quietly, deeply absorbed in thought and staring into vacancy for a long while. But it's really terrible, he added, suddenly getting up to go to bed. And I have no-one to talk to any more, he sighed. Eva, of course, but that was not what I had in mind.

What he had in mind was that other conversation, the running conversation, which had always meant so much to Elias Rukla. It is possible that some men have such a relationship with their wife, or the woman in their life, that the running conversation can be had with her, but for Elias Rukla that had never seemed natural; his connection with her who was his wife was quite different and did not at all correspond to Elias Rukla's need for a running conversation, nor, on second thoughts, could he see that the married couples he knew behaved in any other way than he and Eva in this matter, though he had to admit that he was possibly making this judgment all too superficially. To Elias Rukla, participating in a conversation had always seemed animating. There were few things that could rouse him more than to have been present at a conversation or discussion, both as it occurred and afterwards when he went home, or had come home and was reflecting on what had been said, sort of developing the argument further and, not least, improving on his own remarks, which were usually few and not always equally good when they were uttered. But this polishing of one's own remarks afterwards was part of it – yes, indeed, it was part of a rich life, Elias Rukla thought, his reflective voice laced with fervour. But, first and foremost, it was the conversation itself that was animating, whether it was carried on as a conversation between two friends, say, at some late hour of the night, or around a table with several participants, some of whom naturally dominated the discussion, while the others stayed more in the background, such as Elias Rukla, but always took a lively interest in what was being said, all but stirred to their depths. Even if you would sit all evening without saying a word, you had been ardently involved, waiting eagerly for the next argument from one of the dominant participants and repeating the words to yourself once they had been spoken, appraisingly, uh-huh, or hmm, or I'll be damned, and without getting an inferiority complex because you had a tendency to agree with the last speaker, the last honourable speaker, and then changed your opinion when the next person said something, for that's the way it is, Elias Rukla thought, fired up as he recalled these conversations he had so often been part of. But now and then it happened that Elias Rukla, too, had arrived at a clear idea, or at any rate something that could become a clear idea, which he was itching to bring up, while at the same time wondering if he dared to, because it could well happen that what now seemed so clear to his mind would appear rather stupid when he gave vent to his opinions in the form of a sentence or a remark, as had often happened and could easily happen again, except that, before Elias Rukla made up his mind, the conversation had taken a new turn and Elias Rukla's idea was no longer of any interest, because it would have had the effect of a straggler in the ongoing conversation – it's important to take the floor at the right moment, Elias Rukla had often concluded when he came home, or was on his way home. Oh, how he longed for evenings like that, evenings he had so often experienced before and that stood out so luminously in his memory. It was one of the privileges of freedom to have been permitted to be part of this. But Elias Rukla no longer carried on such conversations, either with one individual, like a staunch friend, or around a table with several others. He no longer had anything to say, nor did it look as though anyone else in his circle of acquaintance, or cultural stratum, had anything to say. They did not seem to be interested in carrying on a conversation any more. In having a real talk, stretching oneself towards an understanding together, whether personal or social, if only for the sake of a brief flash of momentary insight. For his part, Elias Rukla had to admit that he was no longer capable of it, he could simply no longer talk. He did not even know how to start a conversation of the sort he had often taken part in before, but yearned to bring it about once more. The few times he had been on the point of starting such a conversation, either in the staff room at the Fagerborg Secondary School or in society, he had not been able to because he had felt it would somehow have appeared 'artificial'. It would have seemed 'affected', well, 'unnatural', even 'pompous', and Elias Rukla was fairly certain that many others felt the same way, and so the 'artificial' aspect had caused conversation in his social set to cease of itself. In reality, it was puzzling that it should be like that. For example, in the staff room at the Fagerborg school there were gathered every day forty to fifty people who, together, were the mainstay of the general knowledge of our time in history, religion, botany, biology, French, German, English, American language and literature, even Spanish, in addition to the Scandinavian languages and literatures, of course, physiology, physics, mathematics, chemistry, art history, economics, political history, sociology, besides physical improvement through athletics and nutrition, and even though none of those who were here were champions in their fields, capable of coming up with new ideas in their disciplines, nevertheless they had sufficient knowledge to keep abreast of and understand new developments in their area of expertise, in any case if one took the large view and was not too critical of the *actual* competence of individual teachers, and no matter what, the amount of knowledge possessed by any individual within his or her discipline was great enough for the authorities to have chosen them all to instruct the coming generation in their fields, and what struck Elias Rukla in that connection as extremely remarkable was the shallow impact left by this stock of knowledge, well, by this high cultural level, on the personality of the individual teacher. Contrary to one's expectations, it looked as if the teachers felt compelled to deny, at all costs, that they found themselves at this high cultural level, which they then could, as a matter of course, use as their point of departure when they voiced an opinion. Instead, they presented themselves as slaves of indebtedness. That was what they talked about, that was the focus of their conversation. Every morning forty to fifty slaves of indebtedness settled down with their lunch packets in the staff room at Fagerborg Secondary School. They chatted about this and that. About the size of their student loans p.t. and p.a., about the size and rate of interest of their housing loans p.t. and p.a., and about the size and terms of repayment of their car loans p.t. and p.a. Not all were p.t. slaves of indebtedness, it was the younger ones who were most deeply in debt; the others, such as individuals of Elias Rukla's age and upwards, were former slaves of indebtedness. In the staff room, face to face with his colleagues, Elias Rukla was first and foremost a freed slave of indebtedness and, to spite his face, expressed himself safely in accordance with that when he said something; that is to say, when he heard a younger colleague state that the rate of interest on student loans was now down to 8 per cent, he could inform him that it was exactly as high, or low, a rate of interest as when he, Elias Rukla, began to pay off his student loan in the year of grace 1970, and he could also tell this same younger colleague about the deep financial dread he had felt shoot through him the first time the rate of interest on his housing loan rose above 10 per cent, in 1982. That's the way it was in the staff room, all talking about their own lives as former or present slaves of indebtedness; that was the favourite topic in the lunch break, and if Elias Rukla met any of them when he socialised, with the wives starchily rigged out and the men dressed in comfortable, modern going-out clothes, it was, worse luck, also in their common capacity as slaves of indebtedness, you bet. There, too. Always in their capacity as slaves of indebtedness, conspicuously so, Elias Rukla thought. Not that he could not understand it – the salary of a senior master was not high, but, on the other hand, these miserably paid colleagues of his also represented something else, a high level of culture, which they did their best to hide so as not to contribute to exposing the 'artificial' aspect of their lives and preferences, not only out of respect for themselves but also for those others who found themselves at the same level. And so, two persons who both exist at a high cultural level would forthwith introduce themselves to one another as slaves of indebtedness and launch into a conversation with this as a starting point, both in the slaves' own venue, the staff room, and when they met in society. It was as though they were able to see themselves as socially conscious individuals, that is, as persons who could talk together about something they had in common and was essential to all who participated in the conversation, only by starting with themselves as slaves of indebtedness. Given their level of culture, they were haunted by a justified fear that, in a social sense, they would appear somewhat 'artificial', even 'unnatural', but as slaves of indebtedness they experienced a virtually dramatic social existence that was well worth commenting and dwelling on both for themselves and others. True, being enslaved by debt you were a loser, a not entirely successful person, but it linked you to social life as a completely modern individual. On the premise of being a slave of indebtedness, you could also throw yourself on the newspapers and the TV programmes and enjoy commenting on what was said there, which, after all, was an expression of the style-setting trends, and as a slave of indebtedness it was not *that* difficult to share the values and preferences, even the attitude towards life, that were expressed there. And Elias Rukla had nothing to say, but he too talked and talked about nothing. Like the rest. Often with a critical and ironic distance to it all, but always about nothing. Elias Rukla remembered that when he had read *The Unbearable Lightness of Being* by Kundera, he had been disappointed. Not by the book, which was excellent, even a masterpiece, but by the title. The title was wrong. The book was not about the unbearable lightness of being, but about something else. For the unbearable lightness of being is not an existential condition of human life as such but a social condition of that life for certain strata of the Western world in the latter half of the twentieth century. The unbearable lightness of being is something which affects brooding people, hungry for knowledge, at Fagerborg Secondary School in the Norwegian capital in the last two decades of our century. And that deprives one of the ability to say anything. To others. To speak. Conversation had come to a standstill. People belonging to Elias Rukla's social stratum no longer talked together. Or only briefly and superficially. They practically shrugged at one another. Maybe *to* one another as well, in a sort of ironic mutual understanding. Because the public space required for a conversation is occupied. There they are otherwise engaged, as the saying goes. Being an outsider and having to proclaim that the public space is occupied, you become 'artificial'. In 'unnatural' amazement you have to state that such a space no longer exists. No longer exists, no longer exists. No longer exists, so that a cultured senior master like Elias Rukla could suddenly hear himself exclaim, Well, if Kaci Kullman Five hasn't gone and got diabetes! I wonder if it can be combined with being a top politician. Why did he say it? Aloud, in the staff room, so that all his colleagues could hear it. Were they open-mouthed with astonishment? No, they were not. On the contrary, they nodded meaningfully. They, too, were wondering. Whether Kaci Kullman Five would manage. To combine. Being a top politician and having diabetes. It certainly was not easy. Oh, how Elias Rukla would at times pine for someone to talk to. Oh, how he longed for someone to break out of this and *say* something, if nothing else than a reference to the fact that life has other things to offer. He was really looking for someone to allude to that, if only in a kind of code – yes, if only someone or other, during one of those quick exchanges in the staff room, would suddenly point his index finger at the heavens and in that way signal that there existed a long religious tradition, based on Christianity, in our part of the world, and that consequently one often pointed straight up like that, towards the heavens, where according to tradition God and his angels, well, the blessed ones too, were supposed to be, for then Elias Rukla would have thrown his arms around his neck, regardless of how ironic such an index finger would have appeared, both to the one who performed this act and to the others. For Elias Rukla it would have been a sign, replete with seriousness, even if just then it had been dressed up in the conventional language of irony. Oh, he was truly underfed; he felt that his brain was overheated, as if his brain membrane were afflicted with a latent spiritual inflammation which might break out at any moment and that, therefore, he no longer could be considered quite sane, as though he were expecting an attack, as though he had a violent, liberating round of vomiting directly ahead of him, in the immediate future, a round that never came. He searched for something in his colleagues that could express this *something else*, something that made an overture possible; he searched high and low in every word they spoke, with the best will in the world to put the most favourable construction on everything and rush to the rescue of the individual in question as soon as the possibly cryptic words had been spoken, in order to show him his gratitude, and then begin to speak himself, most likely a mere hoarse whisper in the first round, he assumed. And it did happen, once. Suddenly it had happened! One of his colleagues came into the staff room just before the bell rang for the first class and said, I'm somewhat of a Hans Castorp today, I should probably have stayed under the eiderdown. A jolt shot through Elias Rukla. Had he heard correctly? Was the name of Hans Castorp mentioned, and in this free and easy way, in passing? Hans Castorp, the main character in Thomas Mann's novel *The Magic Mountain*, referred to by a senior master at Fagerborg Secondary School, and not by a German teacher, but actually by someone who taught mathematics! Yes, it was true, and to Elias Rukla this was a shining moment. Here it must be interjected that it was not the first time, of course, that names of authors or fictional characters were mentioned among his colleagues at Fagerborg Secondary School. This happened quite frequently – Ibsen, Duun, Kielland, and so on – but in that case in a pedagogical context, regarding problems that had to do with teaching. Or someone had been to the National Theatre and seen an Ibsen play, and then, of course, Ibsen's name came up, and often also the most important characters in the play, besides the names of the actors that appeared in the roles in question. But in that case it was more in the nature of a ritual: a colleague had had a delightful evening at the theatre and mentioned it in the staff room, and maybe another colleague had been at the same theatre a few days earlier and seen the same piece, and the latter might then also mention it, if he had not done so previously, and you might even hear a certain disagreement being expressed concerning whether So-and-so's interpretation of the role of Hedda Gabler, or Miss Wangel, was convincing or not. They were brief exchanges, expresssed in the same way as comments on whether Jahn Otto Johansen's beard was a disturbing element in TV's Foreign Magazine or not, or whether Dan Børge Akerø's style as a presenter was his own or had resulted from painstaking study of foreign models, especially from the USA, or England maybe. But the remark by the mathematics teacher, I'm somewhat of a Hans Castorp today, was a different matter. It was a naive and natural remark which had simply escaped his colleague's lips without his giving it much thought. No profundity, just a mathematics teacher who felt a touch of fever and had therefore wondered whether he should stay at home today, under his eiderdown, or whether to forget about it and go to school anyway, because after all he only felt a bit limp and not really sick, and so he wanted his colleagues to know about it, that he didn't feel quite alright, and the moment he was going to do just that, it occurred to him that his condition was, after all, a bit like the one that Hans Castorp experienced in *The Magic Mountain*, throughout its eight to nine hundred pages, and so he said it, as an allusion which would explain his condition, not to evoke sympathy, but to define his condition with a common reference that simply occurred to him – I'm somewhat of a Hans Castorp today, I should probably have stayed under the eiderdown – and perhaps he was reading *The Magic Mountain* just then and had thought, when he awoke with a bit of fever, that today I'll stay home and lie under the eiderdown so I can continue to read *The Magic Mountain*, but then he had changed his mind, and to explain that he had said, I'm somewhat of a Hans Castorp today, I should have stayed under the eiderdown, and the moment he said it, one of his colleagues, the fifty-odd-years-old Norwegian and history teacher Elias Rukla, began to tremble, for joy. Yes, a thrill of joy shot through him. Another human being, a colleague at that, had mentioned the fictional character Hans Castorp by name, as a natural reference to his own general condition! It was a strange schoolday for Elias Rukla. His joy remained with him all day, when he stood at his desk teaching and, afterwards, when he dropped into the staff room and sat there with his colleagues, glancing discreetly over at the colleague who had said this. He sat behind his desk and conducted his class in his somnolent way, an average grey class that failed to rise above the merely routine in the way he presented the literature of his mother tongue, but his heart was singing all the while: I'm somewhat of a Hans Castorp today, I'm somewhat of a Hans Castorp today, and this joy was so intense that he passed his hand over his forehead to find out whether he, too, wasn't a little sweaty, a little damp, with an ever-so-little trace of fever today. For a long time afterwards Elias Rukla's attention was directed at this colleague. He would very much like to become better acquainted with him. Well, actually he forced himself on him, but without his colleague noticing. Sat down beside him in the brief breaks (in the noon break, at the lunch hour, they had more or less permanent seats, and Elias Rukla sat at a different table from this maths teacher) and waited for him to say something. Something like what he had said, something that could give him that same remarkable uplift. Met him constantly in the narrow corridor where the teachers had their private cabinets, standing beside him there. Tried to say something himself. But what should he say? What he wished to say he could not bring himself to say, and what he actually said did not lead to their becoming better acquainted, just a few simple, casual words uttered to avoid a complete silence as they stood like this beside each other in the narrow passage, or sat at the same table in one of the brief breaks. He thought he might invite him for dinner! Featuring Eva's lamb roast, with garlic and rosemary. No, not garlic, it wouldn't do to invite strangers and serve them food that contained garlic; there were always some people who did not appreciate that, because of their breath afterwards. No, lamb roast with parsley, lots of parsley. He would invite the colleague and his wife for dinner, at home with Eva and himself. He stood in the narrow passage in front of their book cabinets, trying to pluck up his courage and invite him for dinner. But wouldn't it sound rather odd? After all, they did not know one another, being simply colleagues with a passing acquaintance who had now begun to exchange a few brief words about nothing in particular. So would it not look a bit peculiar to invite him for dinner, together with his wife at that? But how about without his wife? Worse still – Eva and Elias Rukla and the maths teacher, why in the world? No, he had to invite him with his wife. But to do so struck him as being so out of place; after all, he did not know his colleague really well, and as for his wife, he did not even know who she was, and Eva of course knew nothing about either of them. Maybe he should invite

Rolfsen too, Rolfsen and his wife, Rolfsen who sat at the same table as the maths teacher in the noon break, directly across from him – he had seen them often talk together, and Rolfsen and his wife knew both Eva and him well; yes, that must be it. But he did not do that either, for when all was said and done he did not think he knew him well enough to invite him and his wife together with Rolfsen and Rolfsen's wife, although they both knew Rolfsen well. He must get to know him better first. But he didn't, being unable to bring himself to say something that could have made them better acquainted, nor was there anything in the behaviour of the maths teacher which could be interpreted to mean that he wished to become better acquainted with Elias Rukla, and besides, as time went on, he found it improper to force himself upon him in that way, without his colleague noticing anything, to be sure, that he was convinced of anyway, and so after a while Elias Rukla stopped both being on the lookout for him in the narrow passage in front of the book cabinets and sitting down at his table in the brief breaks, doing it only now and then when it seemed quite natural and otherwise never again. But he was constantly waiting. For his colleague to say something that would make Elias Rukla tremble for joy and go into a sweat, as in a mild fever; he was listening with half an ear sitting there, but, of course, there is so much noise in the staff room, especially during the noon break, that as a rule it is impossible to hear what people at other tables are saying, especially when you do not make an effort to listen but only sit there, inadvertently prepared in case something should happen, which was not very likely. Oh, how he pined for someone to talk to. Also in the evening when he sat at home in the living room in Jacob Aalls gate, with his beer and his shots of aquavit, occupied with his own thoughts after Eva had gone to bed. He had his own ideas and read a lot. History and novels. He mostly read novels of the 1920s, which were a concept to him: Marcel Proust, Franz Kafka, Hermann Broch, Thomas Mann, and Musil were the authors he liked to read, and they were all authors of the 1920s to him. Also James Joyce, though he did not like him, but all the same he considered him a 1920s author, because that way you could perceive the broad outlines of the twentieth-century European novel. Strictly speaking, few of his 1920s authors were actually authors of the 1920s, in any case not without considerable reservations. Like Kafka. Kafka did not write a single book in the 1920s, most of what he wrote appeared even before 1914, but who is more of a 1920s author than Kafka? And Thomas Mann was originally a nineteenth-century author, but his great books, *The Magic Mountain* and *Doctor Faustus,* were novels of the 1920s, despite the fact that *Doctor Faustus* was actually published after World War Two. And Marcel Proust's *In Search of Lost Time* – most of that work was written before 1914 and very little in the 1920s. But it is the 1920s that have given them their *character,* not only because most of the works of these writers were published then, and attracted attention then, but because it was felt so right that they are placed in the 1920s, when one considers that, for five whole years, the old Europe was going under in a futile, purposeless, and utterly ruthless bloodbath in the muddy trenches of Flanders. That Europe survived that war is the truly historical riddle of our century, which must be understood at one time or another, in any case by me, Elias Rukla thought. And these novels of the 1920s, as Elias Rukla's conceived of them, are stimulating also because they do not differ from one another according to whether they were actually written before 1914, during the Great War of 1914–18, or after it, in the actual 1920s, like *The Magic Mountain*, or for that matter later, in the 1930s or 1940s – indeed, Elias Rukla could point to novels written up to our own time that he would not hesitate to call novels of the 1920s. *The Trial, The Guermantes Way, The Sleepwalkers, The Man Without Qualities, The Magic Mountain* (and also *Ulysses*, if you will, though it is a dead end, Elias Rukla insisted stubbornly to himself), they are all hypnotic, soberly descriptive novels of the same historical domain, our century at the point in time where truth has become clear and painful. Why Elias Rukla was so taken with the novels of the 1920s, he did not know; he could not recognise himself in them, if that is what one would suppose, but he liked their style and temperature, how-ever much the individual 1920s authors differed among themselves, both in style and temperature. What he found again were the mental jolts caused by the great European war, found again in his own mind eighty years later. His own country had been a neutral outskirt during that war, in any case as far as the Flanders trenches were concerned, and yet his innermost being belonged to the regions where these jolts were still reverberating, and this is something that more people than I ought to have reflected upon, Elias Rukla thought, both the fact that the 1920s can be found before the *cause* of the 1920s, the 1914-18 war, and that the jolts from it can be found in my mind, despite the absence of historical documentation, Elias Rukla thought, slightly puzzled. Perhaps I ought to include Kundera, too, as a 1920s author, though I've previously refused to do so, because his work is so marked by another postwar era, Eastern Europe after 1945, and not by the 1914–18 war, but judging by what I am saying now, that should not be a hindrance, if I am to use myself as reader as an example, and that, of course, I must be allowed to do, and then, figuratively speaking, Kundera will fit in perfectly as a 1920s author, and since I value him so highly and all – yes, I do, thought Elias Rukla – Kundera is also an author of the 1920s. But of the old 1920s authors he gradually came to like Mann the best. At first it had been Kafka, then Marcel Proust, but lately he had begun to like Thomas Mann more and more. And that was because he had a curious idea that Thomas Mann was the only author who could have written a novel about him, Elias Rukla, and that he could have written down his entire narrative without self-pity, without whining, and with a rare irony, completely different from the kind of irony which is fashionable in our time, the Mannian irony, which is not used as a defence against reality but is a discreet hint that, when all is said and done, as eventually happens, this fate too (in this imagined instance, that of Elias Rukla) is rather unimportant, though it certainly is a fate and as such must be studied, as it certainly can be. To qualify oneself for being the central character in a novel is, of course, an achievement in itself, and with what right do I imagine I can be seen as such a character, and in a novel by Thomas Mann at that? Elias Rukla thought, on the verge of shaking his head at himself. Thomas Mann would not have been interested in my soul, or in my soul's darkness, by itself, and why in the world should he take any interest in it? But I imagine that he might have derived a certain pleasure from describing my wanderings across the floor tonight, in my apartment in Jacob Aalls gate, where I'm walking back and forth, plagued by the fact that I am a socially aware individual who no longer has anything to say, Elias Rukla thought. Actually, Thomas Mann was the only writer of the 1920s who would at all have considered an offer from Elias Rukla to turn him into a character in a novel. He could vividly imagine turning up for an audition to be selected as a fictional character and being scrutinised by the novelists of the 1920s. He could see how they declined with thanks, one after another, he saw Marcel Proust barely raise an eyelid before casting a brief, meaningful, ironic glance at his colleagues, before Céline's coarse laughter (yes, Céline is also an author of the 1920s, a typical one, though *Journey to the End of the Night* was written in the thirties) resounded in Elias Rukla's ears. Only Thomas Mann would take the poor candidate aspiring to be a fictional character seriously.

He would have looked at Elias Rukla and asked if he could, in a few words, say why he was of the opinion that precisely his fate was suitable as fictional material, either in the capacity of a central character or a minor figure, for, after all, if one has the ambition to be a central character, one must have a clear understanding that one can also be suitable as a minor character – that is a condition which must be agreed to before any author will take the slightest interest in one's fate, he thought Thomas Mann would have said to him. And after Elias Rukla had given an account of his life – and that would, whether I stammered or not, be a model of brevity, he thought – Thomas Mann would give him a reserved but friendly look, he thought, and say, Well, I can't promise anything, as there is no way I can fit you and your life into my present plans, as far as I can see, but there will be other times after this, and then we can possibly come back to the matter. I don't promise anything, quite the contrary, yet it should be sufficient to keep you from being discouraged and make you continue your life as before, even if you should not be granted the privilege of entering one of my novels, as a character. Well, this is how Elias Rukla had spent evening after evening, staying up late fantasising, a bit shyly, about his own life and its possibility of at least making contact with the literature he valued most of all, well, perhaps also a bit shame-facedly, because he was afraid he was putting too big words into the mouth of Thomas Mann in the matter of judging whether he was suitable as a character in one of his novels, or that it would not do for him, even if only in his thoughts, to have Thomas Mann express an opinion about his possibilities as a character in one of Thomas Mann's own novels. We were now far into the 1990s and, dazzled by modernity, Norwegians had already begun to look forward with eagerness to the millennium and the presumed spectacular fireworks that would mark the occasion, Elias Rukla thought with a barely audible sigh.

After Eva Linde's daughter, Camilla Corneliussen, had moved out of the apartment in Jacob Aalls gate, only the two of them were left there. A rather sottish senior master and his wife, a former beauty. Could it be said that Eva Linde's indescribable beauty had disintegrated? To Elias Rukla this was not the correct way of expressing it. He could say, perhaps, that her beauty was gone, or that she had lost her beauty, but in that case he had to leave out the notion of 'indescribable' from her former beauty, because he would have perceived it as quite inadequate, even misleading, to say that Eva Linde's indescribable beauty was gone, or that she had lost her indescribable beauty. Eva Linde could not lose her indescribable beauty. The biologically conditioned change that had taken place with her had to be described otherwise than with reference to what had been the very sign of the beauty she had once possessed. What he could have said, and he did say to himself, in his heart, was that he had difficulty retrieving Eva Linde's charm in the figure and behaviour she now appeared to him in and with. She had become quite filled out and, in consequence, she could appear rather heavy. That is, she moved in a different way through the room now than at the time he had got to know her, and when he heard her footsteps he often came to think of that. Her face had also lost that softness which had undeniably distinguished it earlier on and helped make her person so attractive to men. But when Elias Rukla saw young women, he thought their faces had a smoothness about them rather than the softness he associated with Eva Linde at the same age, which he had to confess he missed. But he missed this softness only by looking at Eva, not at young women. Eva would sit before the mirror applying her make-up as before. Elias Rukla noticed that she could see her own drawn face, where the refined features had disappeared and, along with them, the line of her throat as she bent over, her hair falling slightly forward, causing her to brush it away as before. As he stood behind her in the doorway to the bedroom, looking at his wife before the mirror of her make-up table, Elias Rukla came out with encouraging comments about woman's everlasting vanity, such as men with exceptionally beautiful wives can often permit themselves by way of a joke, as though nothing had befallen her. He felt obliged to come out with such comments, though as a matter of fact it had not been necessary. True, Eva Linde tried as best she could to repair her faded appearance, but she did not seem to mind very much that things had gone the way they had. What had happened had happened. On the whole, she appeared relieved, if anything, that her beauty was gone. She let the wrinkles and the creases emerge without the least sign of hysteria at having lost the lightness and the indefinable charm that had previously been inextricably associated with her person. For that matter, she had never understood her own beauty, viewing it as a fortuitous attribute of herself, and had felt bothered rather than flattered by men's glances on account of this fortuitousness. Now she was liberated from it, and it seemed to agree with her. When Elias Rukla now stood behind her on the threshold to the bedroom and remarked upon her 'vanity' as she was making her toilet as usual, she had to smile; she liked the fact that he was doing it, but it had not been necessary, he did not keep up her spirits by doing so.

Already, before Camilla moved out, Eva Linde had decided on a new future. She left her job as a secretary at the Oslo Cinemas because she wanted to study to become a social worker. Elias had supported her in this, for she had a strong desire for more meaningful work than she felt she was doing at the Oslo Cinemas, or as a secretary in general. So she began to take a number of watches at various institutions, especially such as had to do with drug addicts. All this to collect points in order to be admitted to Norway's College of Municipal and Social Affairs. Elias Rukla found it a bit difficult to understand her sudden interest in drug addicts, she had never expressed it before, but it may have been related to Camilla's youth and her fear, as a mother, that her daughter might, through bad luck or a quest for excitement, end up in milieus that turned young people into drug addicts almost before they knew it themselves. But she had not expressed a specific fear of that kind, nor, as far as they knew, had Camilla given her any grounds for it. Elias himself was of the opinion that, mainly, she was no longer satisfied with her work as a secretary and did not want to continue with it, especially when envisaged as something she was to do for decades ahead, and that she was therefore more or less looking for something new and then, more or less by chance, hit on the idea of becoming a social worker, because the work with drug addicts looked exciting to her, an impression which must have been confirmed by her daily association with them for two or three years as a substitute, since she had not given it up and started something else, or for that matter anything at all, which she had also had the possibility to do, as Elias Rukla's homebound wife, in any case theoretically. Why working with drug addicts could appear exciting and challenging to her, Elias Rukla was at a loss to understand; to him it looked like a heavy grind, with few bright spots, in a milieu that could scarcely make anyone feel jolly, as Elias had gathered when Eva came home from her watches – from night-watches early in the morning, for example. But the fact was that she preferred it to being a secretary, and without hesitation, even when she came home physically worn out and psychologically exhausted after a night-watch. Elias Rukla suspected there was a connection between Eva's loss of interest in working as a secretary and the fading of her beauty. This was not exactly the sort of theory that he would air to others, least of all Eva herself. But at the time when she was indescribably beautiful, she had been happy as a secretary, and that was, Elias Rukla suspected, because her beauty gave her a kind of protection. Against men's glances, however paradoxical that might sound. Her beauty had an educational effect on men who entered the office, where she sat behind the counter. On most, in any case. They became friendly and polite in their whole manner when they saw her, pulling themselves together somehow and making the utmost effort to be courteous, matter-of-fact and informative as far as their business was concerned. She had liked that. And those who did not, those who tried to get fresh with her, puffing themselves up and ruffling their feathers, did so in a situation where they made themselves look utterly absurd and could easily be ridiculed by a pointed or rude rejoinder from Eva's mouth, often in the presence of another secretary or a male superior. Those fugitive glances that Eva otherwise had had to endure, which she could never get the better of, those furtive sidelong glances which she felt in her back and never could stare down, she finally could put paid to and get even for in the office of the Oslo Cinemas, to her great delight. Elias felt he had a basis for maintaining this in light of what Eva had told him about her work. But when her beauty faded, without her showing any bitterness incidentally, this pleasure disappeared, and all that remained was just routine office work; consequently, she looked for something else, something more rewarding, and she chose to become a social worker and take watches, and she had never regretted it. This very autumn, only three weeks ago, she had started at Norway's College of Municipal and Social Affairs, after receiving the happy news early in the summer that she had been accepted. That meant that Eva Linde, who was now in her late forties, had a demanding three-year college course ahead of her. It also meant that he and Eva had to manage for the duration on one income, his teacher's salary, which was not overly high but high enough to allow them to cope fairly well if they were thrifty and observed a sober lifestyle. In any case, Elias was pleased that he had a wife who, in her late forties, had made up her mind to provide herself with a good and, in her eyes, meaningful education, instead of going around being unsatisfied with her work, whether as a secretary or as – and this would have been absurd – a homebound teacher's wife. Incidentally, he had often proposed, from the very moment they were married, in the mid-1970s, that she should resume her studies, but then there had been so many ifs and buts, what with Camilla and one thing and another, that half of it would have sufficed, Elias Rukla had thought.

Eva Linde lived her life in the apartment on Jacob Aalls gate, lying asleep behind the bedroom door as Elias Rukla sat up in the evening with his own thoughts. She went early to bed to be rested the next day, which for her included studies at the Social College, where her fellow students mostly belonged to a much younger generation than she did. Despite the fact that her beauty had badly faded, she was still an elegant lady. She knew how to dress, whether she went around in blue jeans, like her fellow students, or turned up in a grey suit and high-heeled shoes. An elegant lady, Elias Rukla could see that, as did also the others. Somewhat filled out, certainly, but an elegant, mature lady. She had, however, lost her charm for Elias Rukla, her husband. There had always been something affected about Eva, which he had loved. She had felt bothered by attracting men's glances because of the way she happened to look, to be sure, but still she had not avoided becoming the prisoner of her own beauty. Though she had disliked the glances directed at her, she could not desist from reacting to them, and that she had done in such a charmingly affected manner. Her fragile beauty. Her whole manner had been based on her being perceived as indescribably beautiful. She had not been able to avoid playing up her beauty, because it was herself, after all, the way the outside world perceived her, and even though she did not regard it as having any value per se, and none at all to her, who of course couldn't help it, her beauty was nonetheless what constituted her value and therefore had to be played up for her to attain any value at all. Forced to maximise her beauty, because she had had nothing else to maximise! And if she had had something else to play up, nobody would have cared about it anyway, at any rate when it came to comprehending her nature and being drawn towards it. She had known her value, in spite of not acknowledging it. When she *looked* at a man, she knew what it meant. She ought, therefore, *not* to look at men, but when she did she knew what it meant. That is, she knew she *could* look at a man and that it would cause, with almost the certainty of a law, the intended effect to occur. A chance thing and ridiculous, but that is how it was. When her beauty was gone, she knew that this would no longer occur automatically and that, consequently, she was spared having to deal with it. She was released from the prison of her beauty. Willy-nilly, she did not have to put on an act. Her beauty was gone and she could be natural. Not an affected woman, but a natural human being. She could appear as a straightforward and simple mature lady who impressed people with her courage and her determination to undertake a prolonged education at her age. Elias too. An elegant lady who wore blue jeans, like her young fellow students, or who could show up in a grey suit and high-heeled shoes whenever convenient, or appropriate to the weather. Her face a bit drawn, as an expression of a natural biological development that overtakes all, men and women alike, but which for a woman often means that she loses her fascination as exceptionally attractive, with often pathetic consequences if she does not realise this but fights it, trying to look like herself as a young girl instead of enjoying her life as shaped by biological rhythms. Elias Rukla could not deny that he was proud of his wife, and he often felt a hidden, but in reality deep, satisfaction to be living by her side, as he had already done for nearly twenty years. But not without missing her charm, or affectation, if you will.

It was a feeling that he could share with no-one. He could not tell Eva, I love your affectation, because she wouldn't have cared whether he said so or not; it would have been a matter of indifference to her. He could have said, I like the way you toss your head right now (because it reminded him of the way the artificial Eva would toss her head, though not entirely, because now she was doing it by force of habit, without any connection at all to the game being played between a captive beauty and the men who were attracted by her, as before, but as a natural toss of her head, which nevertheless brought things back, reminding Elias of something he was searching for), and she would have liked it, although she would not have repeated her movement so that he would say it once more and she could hear him say it. For she was liberated from this now. But he missed what she had been liberated from and, in a strange way, felt it showed callousness on her part that he could not give expression to it.

All in all, Elias Rukla could not help catching himself thinking that Eva Linde's naturalness had a callous tinge to it. Release from affectation showed sides to her suggestive of both indifference and greed. It was as though the demands beauty had made on her demeanour had tamed her natural inclinations. Perhaps there had always been these sides to her, without Elias Rukla seeing it, dazzled as he had been by her charm? What he had called being 'spoiled' or 'pampered' was perhaps an expression of precisely this, but when it appeared in a beautiful woman in her early thirties, say, it made a different, less direct impression than now, when the same appeared in a middle-aged lady close to fifty years old. On the other hand, it was quite clear that, insofar as Eva Linde freed herself from the tyranny of her own beauty, not unaided, but with the help of nature, one might say, this offered her the possibility of displaying her more vulgar sides, with the greatest pleasure at that, without having to pretend, but letting it all come out, unrestrainedly, like a natural human being. There could be no doubt that she was covetous. The way she would look at things owned by others with her drawn face showed a voracity that at times, quite simply, had a frightening effect on Elias Rukla, considering that he shared bed and board with her. Not the greed per se, but what it expressed and pointed to as far as their relationship was concerned. She was obsessed with things she did not herself own. When they were at a party she would loudly admire the hosts' most exquisite articles, going back to look at them time and again and praising them in a loud voice, and the look she then cast at them was full of envy, something that was obviously appreciated by the hosts and made Elias Rukla set his mind at rest for a moment with the thought that she no doubt was doing it as a matter of politeness. But that wasn't true. For she stood in exactly the same way when staring into the display windows of expensive boutiques for women's clothes or exclusive furniture stores. She would stand there staring greedily at the luxury goods within. But she did not reproach him because they could not get these things for themselves. She did, however, show her greed for them, and when the greed lighted up her worn face and she stood there with her heavy, slightly overweight figure – to be sure, in her elegant grey suit – pressing her nose against the shop windows, it had a frightening effect on him. This glorious, no, uproarious female desire in a woman who did not play up her femininity but was simply an unaffected lady in her late forties. This craving for luxury that could never be satisfied and that, except when she peeked in someone else's home or at the window displays, was never expressed as a wish for something she herself wanted to possess. Faced with this unaffected human being, who had renounced relating to her feminine artificiality but harboured such a voracious female desire, Elias Rukla was struck by a dreadful sense of estrangement, and he longed for what had been. Back to her graceful ways, which had captivated him as a matter of course and had therefore been a legitimate reason why he, Elias Rukla, could be close to her, but when she stood there, heavy-set and greedily staring, her nose flattened against the shop windows of luxury boutiques, he had in that moment no legitimate reason to be with her, and it was in the form of moments that this estrangement occurred to him. But at the same time he was struck by how dependent he had become on her, because when she stood there, craving all that luxury she did not express a single wish to obtain for herself, from him, but which she showed him she was fervently dreaming about all the same, even though she did not want it because it was impossible, he knew that, if she did not soon show him a bit of friendliness and trust that could offset this spectacle, well, the suspicion that this was the true expression of her real life, or that this greed for luxury was just a corner of this secret life that was turned away from him, but that she now all but demonstratively displayed to him, then his uneasiness vis-à-vis her would really destroy him. Was she sorry? As she stood there with her nose flattened against the window, an elegant, but rather drawn and flabby, wife in her forties?

But she did show him much kindness, just as he had tried to rise above his ingrained social suffering and show her both respect and kindness. Though they might be moving about in separate worlds, it was in one and the same apartment, and the things that were there they shared, and they associated under these circumstances without colliding but moved past each other in their separate orbits, without the other's presence being felt as an intrusion, a disturbance, or as unpleasant. She would also sometimes suddenly break out of her friendly orbit and turn to him in complete confidence. She had turned forty-seven this autumn, and he was, until today, a senior master, now fifty-three. She took him into her confidence, which gave him a glimpse of the most intimate aspects of her life. She initiated him into her bodily afflictions and, while doing so, pointed at the spots where her afflictions manifested themselves on her body. When she sat thus, half naked, pointing at her varicose veins, she was anything but an elegant lady – that she became only when she put on her blue jeans, which made her look round, or her grey suit and her high-heeled shoes. But she gave him a glimpse of this body of hers with the utmost confidence and naturalness. At those moments he was her husband. Without worrying about the decline that had taken place in her body with regard to voluptuousness, sensuality, etc., she displayed it to him, only to him, as the only eyewitness, while chattering innocently about what bothered her. To Elias this was painful. She was a trifle fat. Flabby. Elias Rukla felt acute pain as he listened to what she was telling him. Pointing at her decaying body, she told him how much her varicose veins bothered her. In a voice that Elias Rukla remembered as it had always addressed him and which, as he remembered, he had felt a special pleasure listening to when he called her on the telephone. They say that even voices change, so that, when you talk to a stranger on the telephone, you can without difficulty determine the person's age; but that doesn't hold true for those we know. If life had turned out differently and Johan Corneliussen and Eva Linde (plus little Camilla) had left for America together in 1974 and remained there, and then had come home for a brief visit after about twenty years and Elias Rukla was to meet them, say, in the lobby of the Hotel Continental, he would have thought, on seeing Eva, That is Eva Linde, but how she has faded! But if instead they had called him and he, after first talking to Johan Corneliussen, got Eva Linde on the line and heard her voice, then he would have thought, Eva! Because he would immediately have recognised her voice, so clear, but with a peculiarly husky undertone, a hoarseness at the lower end of the vocal cords, as though she had a permanent cold, and he would at once have visualised Eva the way he, in this instance, remembered her from the last time he saw her, in May 1974. And it was exactly that voice which Eva spoke with now, as she sat there half naked, displaying the varicose veins on the legs of her rather flaccid body. At that moment he felt a great tenderness for her. Eva! Eva! he thought, standing motionless beside her as this tenderness overwhelmed him. He could probably have expressed this tenderness for Eva, and perhaps he even ought to have done so, but he could not have expressed what was the basis of the tenderness he was now feeling for the somewhat well-filled-out Eva Linde, his wife, because she was unconcerned about, maybe puzzled by, perhaps even averse to that basis, and that way she was also, no doubt, unconcerned about, maybe puzzled by, even perhaps averse to his real feelings for her altogether, Elias Rukla had thought.

Her indifference towards him. It never failed to occupy him. Her possible indifference towards him. For although she showed him the most profound confidence, all but innocent in its sincerity, there was always a possible indifference in everything she did vis-à-vis her husband. How could she not let it worry her that her beauty was gone! Had it not occurred to her that now Elias Rukla was losing the very thing which had drawn him towards her? Even if that were not true, she must nevertheless have feared in her heart that this was the case. That what had attracted Elias to her was about to disappear, for good. It must at any rate have occurred to her, like a shadow across her face at least, but he never saw a hint of such a shadow. That she could take it so lightly! As a liberation on her part, whereby, however, she shut herself up towards him. Did she not understand that? He hoped she did not understand it, that it was so remote from her range of ideas that the thought had not even occurred to her, for if that was not the case, and she knew it, and still was not troubled by it, then it must mean that, to her, it did not matter very much whether he loved her or not and that, in a sense, it had never mattered, but that she was still grateful because, at a time when she was hard-pressed, she could come to him and stay there. Was that the truth of the matter? Because of thoughts like this, Eva Linde continued to appear as an enigmatic, even provocative, woman to Elias Rukla. This rather plump lady with whom he shared bed and board, but who had never opened her innermost self to him and who had not let him in either, with *his* innermost self, his burning questions, neither then nor now, when they were burnt-out questions. And it was her he was thinking of now, standing at the Bislett traffic circle, his hand bloody (ridiculous) from the ribs of the umbrella and himself at his wits' end, not knowing which way to turn as he stood in the light rain that made little splashes of mud for the passing cars. The disaster had occurred. He knew that the principal would attempt to trivialise the whole affair and have the support of the faculty, who would attempt to persuade him to continue by saying that this was something that could have happened to anyone. But it had not happened to just anyone. It had happened to him, and for him it meant that he had fallen out. Fallen out of society, quite simply. He knew he would never again set foot in Fagerborg Secondary School. Not in any other school either, in his capacity as a teacher. How, then, would she who was his wife be able to cope? She who had just started a three-year education at the College of Social Affairs and depended on his income? For this means it's all over, he thought. It is dreadful, but there is no going back.